TRUCKERS

TRUCKERS
TERRY PRATCHETT

**Delacorte
Press**

Published by
Delacorte Press
Bantam Doubleday Dell Publishing Group, Inc.
666 Fifth Avenue
New York, New York 10103

This edition was first published in Great Britain by
Doubleday, a division of Transworld Publishers Ltd.

Library of Congress Cataloging in Publication Data

Pratchett, Terry.
    Truckers / by Terry Pratchett.
        p.   cm.
    Summary: Reluctant to believe that there's a world outside
the department store in which they live, Torrit, Dorcas,
and the other nomes look to Masklin, a newly arrived
"outsider," to lead them to a safe haven when the store
goes out of business.
    ISBN 0-385-29984-2
    [1. Gnomes—Fiction. 2. Department stores—Fiction.
    3. Fantasy.]
    I. Title.
PZ7.P8865Tr   1990   89-34958
[Fic]—dc20   CIP   AC

Manufactured in the United States of America
February 1990
10 9 8 7 6 5 4 3 2 1

BVG

TRUCKERS

CONCERNING
NOMES AND TIME

Nomes are small. On the whole, small creatures don't live for a long time. But perhaps they do live *fast*.

Let me explain.

One of the shortest-lived creatures on the planet Earth is the adult common mayfly. It lasts for one day. The longest-living things are bristlecone pine trees, at 4,700 years and still counting.

This may seem tough on mayflies. But the important thing is not how long your life is, but how long it seems.

To a mayfly a single hour may last as long as a century. Perhaps old mayflies sit around complaining about how life this minute isn't a patch on the good old minutes of long ago, when the world was young and the sun seemed so much brighter and larvae showed you a bit of respect. Whereas the trees, which are not famous for their quick reactions, may just have time to notice the way the sky keeps flickering before the dry rot and wood-worm set in.

It's all a sort of relativity. The faster you live, the more time stretches out. To a nome a year lasts as long as ten years does to a human. Remember it. Don't let it concern you. They don't. They don't even know.

One

I. There was the Site.

II. And Arnold Bros. (est. 1905) Moved upon the face of the Site, and Saw that it had Potential.

III. For it was On High Street.

IV. Yea, it was also Handy for the Buses.

V. And Arnold Bros. (est. 1905) said, Let there be a Store, And Let it be a Store such as the World has not Seen hitherto;

VI. Let the Length of it be from Palmer Street even unto the Fish Market, and the Width of It, from High Street right Back to Disraeli Road;

VII. Let it be High even Unto Five Stories plus Basement, and bright with Elevators; let there be the Eternal Fires of the Boiler Room *in* the Subbasement and, above all other floors, let there be Customer Accounts to Order All Things;

VIII. For this must be what all shall Know of Arnold Bros. (est. 1905): *All Things Under One Roof.* And it shall be called: the Store of Arnold Bros. (est. 1905).

IX. And Thus it Was.

X. And Arnold Bros. (est. 1905) divided the Store into Departments, of Ironmongri, Corsetri, Modes, and others After their Kind, and Created Humans to fill them with *All Things,* saying, Yea, *All Things* Are Here. And Arnold Bros. (est. 1905) said, Let there be Trucks, and Let their Colors be Red and Gold, and Let them Go Forth so that All May Know Arnold Bros. (est. 1905), By Appointment, delivers *All Things;*

XI. Let there be Santa's Grottoes and Winter Sales and Summer Bargains and Back to School Week and All Commodities in their Season;

XII. And into the Store came the Nomes, that it would be their Place, for Ever and Ever.

—*From The Book of Nome, Basements v. I–XII*

This is the story of the Going Home.

This is the story of the Critical Path.

This is the story of the truck roaring through the sleeping city and out into the country lanes, smashing through streetlamps and swinging from side to side and shattering shop windows and rolling to a halt when the police chased it. And when the baffled men went back to their car to report *Listen, will you listen? There isn't anyone driving it!*, it became the story of the truck that started up again, rolled away from the astonished men, and vanished into the night.

But the story didn't end there.

It didn't start there either.

The sky rained dismal. It rained humdrum. It rained the kind of rain that is so much wetter than normal rain, the kind of rain that comes down in big drops and splats, the kind of rain that fills the air from side to side, the kind of rain that is merely an upright sea with slots in it.

It rained a tattoo on the old hamburger boxes and french-fry papers in the wire basket that was giving Masklin a temporary hiding place.

Look at him. Wet. Cold. Extremely worried. And four inches high.

The litter basket was usually a good hunting ground, even in winter. There were often a few cold fries in the wrapping, sometimes even a chicken bone. Once or twice there had been a rat too. It had been a really good day when there had last been a rat—it had kept them going for a week. The trouble was that you could get pretty fed up with rat by the third day. By the third mouthful, come to that.

Masklin scanned the truck parking lot.

And here it came, right on time, crashing through the puddles and pulling up with a hiss of brakes.

He'd watched this truck arrive every Tuesday and Thursday morning for the last four weeks. He timed the driver's stop carefully.

They had exactly three minutes. To someone the size of a nome that's more than half an hour.

He scrambled down through the greasy paper, dropped out of the bottom of the basket, and ran for the bushes at the edge of the park where Grimma and the old folk were waiting.

"It's here!" he said. "Come on!"

They got to their feet, groaning and grumbling. He'd taken them through this dozens of times. He knew it wasn't any use to shout. They just got upset and confused, and then they'd grumble some more. They grumbled about cold fries, even when Grimma warmed them up. They moaned about rat. He'd seriously thought about leaving alone, but he couldn't bring himself to do it. They needed him. They needed someone to grumble at.

But they were too *slow*. He felt like bursting into tears.

He turned to Grimma instead.

"Come *on,*" he said. "Give them a prod or something. They'll never get moving!"

She patted his hand.

"They're frightened," she said. "You go on. I'll bring them out."

There wasn't time to argue. Masklin ran back across the soaking mud of the parking lot, un-slinging the rope and grapnel. It had taken him a week to make the hook, out of a bit of wire teased off a fence, and he'd spent days practicing; he was already swinging it around his head as he reached the truck's wheel.

The hook caught the tarpaulin high above him at the second try. He tested it once or twice, and then, his feet scrabbling for a grip on the tire, pulled himself up.

He'd done it before. Oh, he'd done it three or four times. He scrambled under the heavy tarpau-lin and into the darkness beyond, pulling out more line and tying it as tightly as possible around one of the ropes that was as thick as his arm.

Then he slid back to the edge and, thank good-ness, Grimma *was* herding the old people across the gravel. He could hear them complaining about the puddles.

Masklin jumped up and down with impatience.

It seemed to take hours. He explained it to them millions of times, but people hadn't been pulled up onto the backs of trucks when they were children and they didn't see why they should start now. Old Granny Morkie insisted that all the men look the other way so that they wouldn't see up her skirts, for example, and old Torrit whimpered so much that Masklin had to lower him again so that Grimma could blindfold him. It wasn't so bad after he'd hauled the first few up, because they were able to help on the rope, but time still stretched out.

He pulled Grimma up last. She was light. They were *all* light, if it came to that. You didn't get rat every day.

It was amazing. They were all on board. He'd worked with an ear cocked for the sound of footsteps on gravel and the slamming of the driver's door, and it hadn't happened.

"Right," he said, shaking with the effort, "that's it, then. Now if we just go—"

"I dropped the Thing," said old Torrit. "The Thing. I dropped it, d'you see? I dropped it down by the wheel when she was blindfoldin' me. You go and get it, boy."

Masklin looked at him in horror. Then he poked his head out from under the tarpaulin and, yes, there it was, far below. A tiny black cube on the ground.

The Thing.

It was lying in a puddle, although that wouldn't affect it. Nothing touched the Thing. It wouldn't even burn.

And then he heard the sound of slow footsteps on the gravel.

"There's no time," he whispered. "There really is no time."

"We can't go without it," said Grimma.

"Of course we can. It's just a, a thing. We won't need the stupid thing where we're going."

He felt guilty as soon as he'd said it, amazed at his own lips for uttering such words. Grimma looked horrified. Granny Morkie drew herself up to her full, quivering height.

"May you be forgiven!" she barked. "What a terrible thing to say! You tell him, Torrit." She nudged Torrit in the ribs.

"If we ain't taking the Thing, I ain't going," said Torrit sulkily. "It's not—"

"That's your leader talkin' to you," interrupted Granny Morkie. "So you do what you're told. Leave it behind, indeed! It wouldn't be decent. It wouldn't be right. So you go and get it, this minute."

Masklin stared wordlessly down at the soaking mud, and then, with a desperate motion, threw the line over the edge and slid down it.

It was raining harder now, with a touch of sleet. The wind whipped at him as he dropped past the great arc of the wheel and landed heavily in the puddle. He reached out and scooped up the Thing—

And the truck started to move.

First there was a roar, so loud that it went beyond sound and became a solid wall of noise. Then there was a blast of stinking air and a vibration that shook the ground.

He pulled sharply on the line and yelled at them to pull him up, and realized that even he couldn't hear his own voice. But Grimma or some-one must have got the idea because, just as the big wheel began to turn, the rope tightened and he felt his feet lifted off the mud.

He bounced and spun back and forth as, with painful slowness, they pulled him past the wheel. It turned only a few inches away from him, a black, chilly blur, and all the time the hammering sound battered at his head.

I'm not scared, he told himself. This is much worse than anything I've ever faced, and it's not frightening. It's too terrible to be frightening.

He felt as though he were in a tiny, warm co-coon, away from all the noise and the wind. I'm going to die, he thought, just because of this Thing, which has never helped us at all, something that's just a lump of stuff, and now I'm going to die and go to the Heavens. I wonder if old Torrit is right about what happens when you die? It seems a bit severe to have to die to find out. I've looked at the sky every night for years and I've never seen any nomes up there. . . .

But it didn't really matter, it was all outside him, it wasn't real—

Hands reached down and caught him under the arms and dragged him into the booming space under the tarpaulin and, with some difficulty, prised the Thing out of his grip.

Behind the speeding truck fresh curtains of gray rain dragged across the empty fields.

And, across the whole country, there were no more nomes.

There had been plenty of them, in the days when it didn't seem to rain so much. Masklin could remember at least forty. But then the highway had come, the stream was put in pipes underground, and the nearest hedges were dug up. Nomes had always lived in the corners of the world, and suddenly there weren't too many corners anymore.

The numbers started going down. A lot of this was due to natural causes, and when you're four inches high, natural causes can be anything with teeth and speed and hunger. Then Pyrrince, who was by way of being the most adventurous, led a desperate expedition *across the highway* one night to investigate the woods on the other side. They never came back. Some said it was hawks, some said it was a truck. Some even said they'd made it halfway and were marooned on the central divider between endless swishing lines of cars.

Then the diner had been built a little farther along the road. It had been a sort of improvement. It depended how you looked at it. If cold leftover fries and scraps of gray chicken were food, then there was suddenly enough for everyone.

And then it was spring, and Masklin looked around and found that there were just ten of them left, and eight of those were too old to get about much. Old Torrit was nearly ten.

It had been a dreadful summer. Grimma organized those who could still get about into midnight raids on the litter baskets, and Masklin tried to hunt.

Hunting by yourself was like dying a bit at a time. Most of the things you were hunting were also hunting *you*. And even if you were lucky and made a kill, how did you get it home? It had taken two days with the rat, including sitting out at night to fight off other creatures. Ten strong hunters could do anything—rob bees' nests, trap mice, catch moles, *anything*—but one hunter by himself, with no one to watch his back in the long grass, was simply the next meal for everything with talons and claws.

To get enough to eat you needed lots of healthy hunters. But to get lots of healthy hunters you needed enough to eat.

"It'll be all right in the autumn," said Grimma, bandaging his arm where a stoat had caught it. "There'll be mushrooms and berries and nuts and everything."

Well, there hadn't been any mushrooms and it had rained so much that most of the berries rotted before they ripened. There were plenty of nuts, though. The nearest hazel tree was half a day's journey away. Masklin could carry a dozen nuts if he smashed them out of their shells and dragged them back in a paper bag from the trash. It took a whole day to do it, risking hawks all the way, and it was just enough food for a day as well.

And then the back of the burrow fell in because of all the rain. It was almost pleasant to get out, then. It was better than listening to the grumbling about his not doing essential repairs. Oh, and there was the fire. You needed a fire at the burrow mouth, both for cooking and for keeping away night prowlers. Granny Morkie went to sleep one day and let it go out. Even she had the decency to be embarrassed.

When Masklin came back that night he looked at the heap of dead ashes for a long time and then stuck his spear in the ground and burst out laughing, and went on laughing until he started to cry. He couldn't face the rest of them. He had to go and sit outside, where, presently, Grimma brought him a shellful of nettle tea. *Cold* nettle tea.

"They're all very upset about it," she volunteered.

Masklin gave a hollow laugh. "Oh, yes, I can tell," he said, "I've heard them. 'You ought to bring back another cigarette butt, boy, I'm right out of tobacco,' and 'We never have fish these days, you might find the time to go down to the river,' and 'Self, self, self, that's all you young people think about, in my day . . .' "

Grimma sighed. "They do their best," she said. "It's just that they don't realize. There were hundreds of us when they were young."

"It's going to take *days* to get that fire lit," said Masklin. They had a lens from a pair of glasses; it needed a very sunny day to work.

He poked aimlessly in the mud by his feet.

"I've had enough," he said quietly. "I'm going to leave."

"But we need you!"

"*I* need me too. I mean, what kind of life is this?"

"But they'll die if you go away!"

"They'll die anyway," said Masklin.

"That's a wicked thing to say!"

"Well, it's true. Everyone dies anyway. *We'll* die anyway. Look at you. You spend your whole time washing and cleaning and cooking and chasing after them. You're nearly three! It's about time you had a life of your own."

"Granny Morkie was very kind to me when I was small," said Grimma defensively. "You'll be old one day."

"You think? And who will be working their fingers to the bone to look after me?"

Masklin found himself getting angrier and angrier. He was certain he was in the right. But it *felt* as if he was in the wrong, which made it worse.

He'd thought about this for a long time, and it had always left him feeling angry and awkward.

All the smart ones and the bold ones and the brave
ones had gone long ago, one way or the other.
Good old Masklin, they'd said, stout chap, you look
after the old folk and we'll be back before you
know it, just as soon as we've found a better place.
Every time good old Masklin thought about this he
got indignant with them for going and with himself for staying. He always gave in, that was his
trouble. He knew it. Whatever he promised himself at the start, he always took the way of least
resistance.

Grimma was glaring at him.

He shrugged.

"All right, all right, so they can come with us,"
he said.

"You know they won't go," she said. "They're
too old. They all grew up around here. They like it
here."

"They like it here when there's us around to
wait on them," muttered Masklin.

They left it at that. There were nuts for dinner.
Masklin's had a maggot in it.

He went out afterward and sat at the top of the
bank with his chin in his hands, watching the highway again.

It was a stream of red and white lights. There
were humans inside those boxes, going about whatever mysterious business humans spent their time
on. They were always in a hurry to get to it, whatever it was.

He was prepared to bet they didn't eat rat. Humans had it really easy. They were big and slow, but they didn't have to live in damp burrows waiting for daft old women to let the fire go out. They never had maggots in their tea. They went wherever they wanted and they did whatever they liked. The whole world belonged to them.

And all night long they drove up and down in these little trucks with lights on. Didn't they ever go to sleep? There must be hundreds of them.

He'd dreamed of leaving on a truck. They often stopped at the diner. It would be easy—well, fairly easy—to find a way onto one. They were clean and shiny, they had to go somewhere better than this. And after all, what was the alternative? They'd never see the winter through here, and setting out across the fields with the bad weather coming on didn't bear thinking about.

Of course he'd never do it. You never actually did it in the end. You just dreamed about following those swishing lights.

And above the rushing lights, the stars. Torrit said the stars were very important. Right at the moment Masklin didn't agree. You couldn't eat them. They weren't even much good for seeing by. The stars were pretty useless when you thought about it. . . .

Somebody screamed.

Masklin's body got to his feet almost before his mind had even thought about it, and he sped silently through the scrubby bushes toward the burrow.

Where, its head entirely underground and its brush waving excitedly at the stars, was a dog fox. He recognized it. He'd had a couple of close shaves with it in the past.

Somewhere inside Masklin's head the part of him that was really him—old Torrit had a lot to say about this part—was horrified to see him snatch up his spear, which was still in the ground where he had plunged it, and stab the fox as hard as he could in a hind leg.

There was a muffled yelp and the animal struggled backward, turning an evil, foaming mask to its tormentor. Two bright yellow eyes focused on Masklin, who leaned panting on his spear. This was one of those times when time itself slowed down and everything was suddenly more real. Perhaps, if you knew you were going to die, your senses crammed in as much detail as they could while they still had the chance. . . .

There were flecks of blood around the creature's muzzle.

Masklin felt himself become angry. It welled up inside him, like a huge bubble. He didn't have much, and this grinning *thing* was taking even that away from him.

As the red tongue lolled out he knew that he had two choices. He could run or he could die.

So he attacked instead. The spear soared from

his hand like a bird, catching the fox in the lip. It screamed and pawed at the wound, and Masklin was running, running across the dirt, propelled by the engine of his anger, and then jumping and grabbing handfuls of rank red fur and hauling himself up the fox's flank to landing astride its neck and drawing his stone knife and stabbing, stabbing, at everything that was wrong with the world. . . .

The fox screamed again and leapt away. If he was capable of thinking then, Masklin would have known that his knife wasn't doing much more than annoying the creature, but it wasn't used to meals fighting back with such fury and its only thought now was to get away. It breasted the embankment and rushed headlong down it, toward the lights of the highway.

Masklin started to think again. The rushing of the traffic filled his ears as he let go and threw himself into the long grass while the creature galloped out onto the asphalt.

He landed heavily and rolled over, all the breath knocked out of him.

But he remembered what happened next. It stayed in his memory for a long time, long after he'd seen so many strange things that there really should have been no room for it.

The fox, as still as a statue in a headlight's beam, snarled its defiance as it tried to outstare ten tons of metal hurtling toward it at seventy miles an hour.

There was a bump, a swish, and darkness.

Masklin lay facedown in the cool moss for a long time. Then, dreading what he was about to see, trying not to imagine it, he pulled himself to his feet and plodded back toward whatever was left of his home.

Grimma was waiting at the burrow's mouth, holding a twig like a club. She spun around and nearly brained Masklin as he staggered out of the darkness and leaned against the bank. He stuck out a weary hand and pushed the stick aside.

"We didn't know where you'd gone," she said, her voice on the edge of hysteria. "We just heard the noise and there it was—you should have been here—it got Mr. Mert and Mrs. Coom and it was digging at the—"

She stopped and seemed to sag.

"Yes, thank you," said Masklin coldly. "I'm all right, thank you very much."

"What—what happened?"

He ignored her and trooped into the darkness of the burrow and lay down. He could hear the old ones whispering as he sank into a deep, chilly sleep.

I should have been here, he thought.

They depend on me.

We're going. All of us.

•

It had seemed a good idea, then.

It looked a bit different, now.

Now the nomes clustered at one end of the great dark space inside the truck. They were silent. There wasn't any *room* to be noisy. The roar of the engine filled the air from edge to edge. Sometimes it would falter and start again. Occasionally the whole truck lurched.

Grimma crawled across the trembling floor.

"How long is it going to take to get there?" she asked.

"Where?" said Masklin.

"Wherever we're going."

"I don't know."

"They're hungry, you see."

They always were. Masklin looked hopelessly at the huddle of old ones. One or two of them were watching him expectantly.

"There isn't anything I can do," he said. "I'm hungry, too, but there's nothing here. It's empty."

"Granny Morkie gets very upset when she's missed a meal," said Grimma.

Masklin gave her a long, blank stare. Then he crawled his way to the group and sat down between Torrit and the old woman.

He'd never really talked to them, he realized. When he was small they were giants who were no concern of his, and then he'd been a hunter among hunters, and this year he'd either been out looking for food or deep in an exhausted sleep. But he

knew Torrit was the leader of the tribe. That stood
to reason, he was the oldest nome. The oldest was
always the leader. That way there couldn't be any
arguments. Not the oldest *woman,* of course, because everyone knew this was unthinkable; even
Granny Morkie was quite firm about that. Which
was a bit odd, because she treated him like an idiot
and Torrit never made a decision without looking
at her out of the corner of his eye. Masklin sighed.
He stared at his knees.

"Look, I don't know how long—" he began.

"Don't you worry about me, boy," said Granny
Morkie, who seemed to have quite recovered.
"This is all rather excitin', isn't it?"

"But it might take ages," said Masklin, "I didn't
know it was going to take this long. It was just a
mad idea. . . ."

She poked him with a bony finger. "Young
man," she said, "I was alive in the Great Winter of
1988. Terrible, that was. You can't tell *me* anything
about going hungry. Grimma's a good girl, but she
worries."

"But I don't even know where we're going!"
Masklin burst out. "I'm sorry!"

Torrit, who was sitting with the Thing on his
skinny knees, peered shortsightedly at him.

"We have the Thing," he said. "It will show us
the Way, it will."

Masklin nodded gloomily. Funny how Torrit
always knew what the Thing wanted. It was just a

black square thing, but it had some very definite ideas about the importance of regular meals and how you should always listen to what the old folk said. It seemed to have an answer for everything.

"And where does this Way take us?" said Masklin.

"You knows that well enough. To the Heavens."

"Oh. Yes," said Masklin. He glared at the Thing. He was pretty certain that it didn't tell old Torrit anything at all; he knew he had pretty good hearing, and he never heard it say anything. It never did anything, it never moved. The only thing it ever did was look black and square. It was *good* at that.

"Only by followin' the Thing closely in all particulars can we be sure of going to the Heavens," said Torrit uncertainly, as if he'd been told this a long time ago and hadn't understood it even then.

"Yes, well," said Masklin. He stood up on the swaying floor and made his way to the tarpaulin. Then he paused to screw up his courage and poked his head under the gap.

There was nothing but blurs and lights and strange smells.

It was all going wrong. It had seemed so sensible that night, a week ago. Anything was better than here, that seemed so obvious then. But it was odd. The old ones moaned like anything when things weren't exactly to their liking, but now, when everything was looking bad, they were almost cheerful.

People were a lot more complicated than they looked. Perhaps the Thing could tell you that, too, if you knew how to ask.

The truck turned a corner and rumbled down into blackness and then, without warning, stopped. He found himself looking into a huge lighted space, full of trucks, full of *humans.* . . .

He pulled his head back quickly and scuttled across the floor to Torrit.

"Er," he said.

"Yes, lad?"

"Heaven. Do humans go there?"

The old nome shook him head. "*The* Heavens," he said. "More than one of 'em, see? Only nomes go there."

"You're absolutely certain?"

"Oh, yes." Torrit beamed. "O' course, they have heavens of their own," he said, "I don't know about that. But they ain't ours, you may depend upon it."

"Oh."

Torrit stared at the Thing again.

"We've stopped," he said. "Where are we?"

Masklin stared wearily into the darkness.

"I think I had better go and find out," he said.

There was whistling outside, and the distant rumble of human voices. The lights went out.

There was a rattling noise, followed by a click, and then silence.

After a while there was a faint scrabbling around the back of one of the silent trucks. A length of line, no thicker than thread, dropped down until it touched the oily floor of the garage.

A minute went by. Then, lowering itself with great care hand over hand, a small, stumpy figure shinnied down the line and dropped onto the floor. It stood rock-still for a few seconds after landing, with only its eyes moving.

It was not entirely human. There were definitely the right number of arms and legs, and the additional parts like eyes and so on were in the usual places, but the figure that was now across the darkened floor in its mouse skins looked like a brick wall on legs. Nomes are so stocky that a Japanese sumo wrestler would look half starved by comparison, and the way this one moved suggested that it was considerably tougher than old boots.

Masklin was in fact terrified out of his life. There was nothing here that he recognized, except for the smell of *all,* which he come to associate with humans and especially with trucks (Torrit had told him loftily that *all* was a burning water that trucks drank, at which point Masklin knew the old nome had gone mad. It stood to reason. Water didn't burn).

None of it made any sense. Vast cans loomed above him. There were huge pieces of metal that had a made look about them. This was definitely a part of a human heaven. Humans liked metal.

He did skirt warily around a cigarette butt, and made a mental note to take it back for Torrit.

There were other trucks in this place, all of them silent. It was, Masklin decided, a truck nest. Which meant that the only food in it was probably *all*.

He untensed a bit and prodded about under a bench that towered against one wall like a house. There were drifts of wastepaper there and, led by a smell that here was even stronger than *all*, he found a whole apple core. It was going brown, but it was a pretty good find.

He slung it across one shoulder and turned around.

There was a rat watching him thoughtfully. It was considerably bigger and sleeker than the things that fought the nomes for the scraps from the litter basket. It dropped on all fours and trotted toward him.

Masklin felt that he was on firmer ground here. All these huge dark shapes and cans and ghastly smells were quite beyond him, but he knew what a rat was all right, and what to do about one.

He dropped the core, brought his spear back slowly and carefully, aimed at a point just between the creature's eyes—

Two things happened at once.

Masklin noticed that the rat had a little red collar.

And a voice said, "Don't! He took a long time to train. Bargains Galore! Where did *you* come from?"

The stranger was a nome. At least Masklin had to assume so. He was certainly nome height and moved like a nome, although he seemed quite young.

But his clothes . . .

The basic color for a practical nome's clothes is mud. That was common sense. Grimma knew fifty ways of making dyes from wild plants and they all yielded a color that was, when you came right down to it, basically muddy. Sometimes yellow mud, sometimes brown mud, sometimes even greenish mud, but still, well, mud. Because any nome who ventured out wearing jolly reds and blues would have a life expectancy of perhaps half an hour before something digestive happened to him.

Whereas this nome was definitely asking to be eaten. He had real shiny boots, not just wooden sandals, on his feet. He had a hat with a feather in it, and a belt that glittered. As for his clothes . . . well, Masklin, who didn't even know what the word *silk* meant, had to assume that this nome was made out of rainbows. As he talked he slapped his leg idly with a leather strap, which, it turned out, was the leash for the rat.

"Well?" he snapped. "Answer me!"

"I came off the truck," said Masklin shortly, eyeing the rat. It stopped scratching its ears, gave him a look, and went and hid behind its master.

"What were you doing on there? Answer me!"

Masklin pulled himself up. "We were traveling," he said.

The nome glared at him. "What's traveling?" he snapped.

"Moving along," said Masklin. "You know? Coming from one place and going to another place."

This seemed to have a strange effect on the nome. If it didn't actually make him polite, at least it took the edge off his tone.

"Are you trying to tell me you came from *Outside?*" he said.

"That's right."

"But that's impossible!"

"Is it?" Masklin looked worried.

"There's nothing Outside!"

"There isn't? Sorry," said Masklin. "But we seem to have come in from it, anyway. Is this a problem?"

"You mean *really* Outside?" said the nome, sidling closer.

"I suppose I do. We never really thought about it. What's this pl—"

"What's it like?"

"What?"

"Outside! What's it like?"

Masklin looked blank. "Well," he said, "it's sort of big—"

"Yes?"

"And, er, there's a lot of it—"

"Yes? Yes?"

"With, you know, things in it—"

"Is it true the ceiling is so high you can't see it?" said the nome, apparently beside himself with excitement.

"Don't know. What's a ceiling?" said Masklin.

"That is," said the nome, pointing up to a gloomy roof of girders and shadows.

"Oh, I haven't seen anything like that," said Masklin. "Outside it's blue or gray, with white things floating around in it."

"And, and, and the walls are such a long way off, and there's a sort of green carpet thing that grows on the ground?" said the nome, hopping from one foot to the other.

"Don't know," said Masklin, even more mystified. "What's a carpet?"

"Wow!" The nome got a grip on himself and extended a shaking hand. "My name's Angalo," he said. "Angalo de Haberdasheri. Haha. Of course that won't mean anything to you! And this is Bobo."

The rat appeared to grin. Masklin had never heard a rat called anything, except perhaps, if you were driven to it, dinner.

"I'm Masklin," he said. "Is it all right if the rest of us come down? It was a long journey."

"Gosh, yes! All from Outside? My father'll never believe it!"

"I'm sorry," said Masklin. "I don't understand. What's so special? We were outside. Now we're inside."

Angalo ignored him. He was staring at the others as they came stiffly down the line, grumbling.

"Old people too!" said Angalo. "And they look just like us! Not even pointy heads or anything!"

"Fresh!" said Granny Morkie. Angalo stopped grinning.

"Madam," he said icily. "Do you know who you're talking to?"

"Someone who's not too old for a smacked bottom," said Granny Morkie. "If I looked just like you, my lad, I'd look a great deal better. Pointy heads, indeed!"

Angalo's mouth opened and shut silently. Then he said, "It's amazing! I mean, Dorcas said that even if there was a possibility of life outside the Store, it wouldn't be life as we know it! Please, please, all follow me."

They exchanged glances as Angalo scurried

away toward the edge of the truck nest but followed him anyway. There wasn't much of an alternative.

"I remember when your old dad stayed out too long in the sun one day. He talked rubbish, too, just like this one," said Granny Morkie quietly.

Torrit appeared to be reaching a conclusion. They waited for it politely.

"I reckon," he said at last, "I reckon we ought to eat his rat."

"You shut up, you," said Granny automatically.

"I'm leader, I am. You've got no right, talking like that to a leader," Torrit whined.

"O' course you're leader," snapped Granny Morkie. "Who said you weren't leader? I never said you weren't leader. You're leader."

"Right." Torrit sniffed.

"And now shut up," said Granny.

Masklin tapped Angalo on the shoulder. "Where *is* this place?" he said.

Angalo stopped by the wall, which towered up into the distance.

"You don't know?" he said.

"We just thought, well, we just *hoped* that the trucks went to—to a good place to be," said Grimma.

"Well, you heard right," said Angalo proudly. "This is the best place to be. This is the Store!"

Two

XIII. And in the Store there was neither Night nor Day, only Opening Time and Closing Time. Rain fell not, *neither* was there Snow.

XIV. And the nomes grew fat and multiplied as the years passed, and spent their time in rivalry and small war, Department unto Department, and forgot all they knew of the Outside;

XV. For they said, Is it not so, Arnold Bros. (est. 1905) has put *All Things* Under One Roof?

XVI. And those who said, Perhaps Not *All* Things, were cruelly laughed at, and prodded.

XVII. And other nomes said, Even were there an Outside, what can it hold that we would need? For here we have the power of the Electric, the Food Hall, and All *manner* of Diversions.

XVIII. And thus the seasons fell thicker than the cushions that are in Soft Furnishings (Third Floor).

XIX. Until a stranger came from afar, crying out in a loud voice, and he cried, Woe, woe.

—From The Book of Nome, First Floor v. XIII–XIX

They tripped over one another, they walked with their heads turned upward and their mouths open, they gawked. Angalo had stopped by a hole in the wall, and waved them through hurriedly.

"In here," he said.

Granny Morkie sniffed.

"That's a rat hole," she said. "You're not asking me to go down a rat hole?" She turned to Torrit. "He's asking me to go down a rat hole! I'm not going down a rat hole!"

"Why not?" said Angalo.

"It's a rat hole!"

"That's just what it looks like," said Angalo. "It's a disguised entrance, that's all."

"Your rat just went through it," said Granny Morkie triumphantly. "I've got eyes. It's a rat hole."

Angalo gave Grimma a pleading look and

ducked through the hole. She poked her head through after him.

"I don't *think* it's a rat hole, Granny," she said in a slightly muffled voice.

"And why is that, pray?"

"Because there's stairs inside. Oh, and nice little lights."

It was a long climb. They had to stop and wait several times for the old ones to catch up, and Torrit had to be helped most of the way. At the top the stairs went through a more dignified sort of door into—

Even when he was young, Masklin had never seen more than forty nomes all together at once.

There were more than that here. And there was food. It didn't look like anything he recognized, but it had to be food. After all, people were eating it.

A space about twice as high as he was stretched away into the distance. Food was stacked in neat piles with aisles among them, and these were thronged with nomes. No one paid much attention to the little group as it shuffled obediently behind Angalo, who had got some of his old swagger back.

Several nomes had sleek rats on leashes. Some of the ladies had mice, which trotted obediently behind them, and out of the corner of his ear Masklin could hear Granny Morkie tut-tutting her disapproval.

He also heard old Torrit say excitedly, "I know

that stuff! That's cheese! There was a cheese sandwich in the basket once, back in the summer of '86,
d'you remember . . . ?" Granny Morkie nudged
him hard in his skinny ribs.

"You shut up, you," she commanded. "You
don't want to show us up in front of all these folk,
do you? Be a leader. Act proud."

They weren't very good at it. They walked in
stunned silence. Fruits and vegetables were stacked
behind trestle tables, with nomes working indus-
triously on them. There were other things, too,
which he couldn't begin to recognize. Masklin
didn't want to show his ignorance, but curiosity
got the better of him.

"What's that thing over there?" he said, pointing.

"It's a salami sausage," said Angalo, "Ever had
it before?"

"Not lately," said Masklin truthfully.

"And they're dates," said Angalo, "And that's a
banana. I expect you've never seen a banana before, have you?"

Masklin opened his mouth, but Granny Morkie
beat him to it.

"Bit small, that one," she said, and sniffed.
"Quite tiny, in fact, compared to the ones we got at
home."

"It is, is it?" said Angalo suspiciously.

"Oh, yes," said Granny, beginning to warm to
her subject. "Very puny. Why, the ones we got at

home"—she paused and looked at the banana, lying on a couple of trestles like a canoe, and her lips moved as she thought fast—"why," she added triumphantly, "we could hardly dig them out o' the ground!"

She stared victoriously at Angalo, who tried to outstare her and gave up.

"Well, whatever," he said vaguely, looking away. "You may all help yourselves. Tell the nomes in charge that it's to go on the Haberdasheri account, will you? But don't say you've come from Outside, I want that to be a surprise."

There was a general rush in the direction of the food. Even Granny Morkie just happened to wander toward it, and acted quite surprised to find her way blocked by a cake.

Only Masklin stayed where he was, despite the urgent complaints from his stomach. He wasn't sure he even began to understand how things worked in the Store, but he had an obscure feeling that if you didn't face them with dignity, you could end up doing things you weren't entirely happy about.

"You're not hungry?" said Angalo.

"I'm hungry," admitted Masklin, "I'm just not eating. Where does all the food *come* from?"

"Oh, we take it from the humans," said Angalo airily. "They're rather stupid, you know."

"And they don't mind?"

"They thinks it's rats," sniggered Angalo. "We

take up rat doodahs with us. At least the Food Hall families do," he corrected himself. "Sometimes they let other people go up with them. Then the humans just think it's rats."

Masklin's brow wrinkled.

"Doodahs?" he said.

"You know," said Angalo. "Droppings."

Angalo nodded. "They fall for that, do they?" he said doubtfully.

"They're very stupid, I told you." The boy walked around Masklin. "You must come and see my father," he said. "Of course it's a foregone conclusion that you'll join the Haberdasheri."

Masklin looked at the tribe. They had spread out among the food stalls. Torrit had a lump of cheese as big as his head, Granny Morkie was investigating a banana as if it might explode, and even Grimma wasn't paying him any attention.

Masklin felt lost. What he was good at, he knew, was tracking a rat across several fields, bringing it down with a single spear throw, and dragging it home. He'd felt really good about that. People had said things like "Well done."

He had a feeling that you didn't have to track a banana.

"Your father?" he said.

"The Duke de Haberdasheri," said Angalo proudly. "Lord Protector of the Mezzanine and Autocrat of the Staff Canteen."

"He's three people?" said Masklin, puzzled.

"Those're his titles. Some of them. He's nearly the most powerful nome in the Store. Do you have things like fathers Outside?"

Funny thing, Masklin thought. He's a rude little twerp except when he talks about the Outside, then he's like an eager little boy.

"I had one once," he said. He didn't want to dwell on the subject.

"I bet you had lots of adventures!"

Masklin thought about some of the things that had happened to him—or, more accurately, had *nearly* happened to him—recently.

"Yes," he said.

"I bet it was tremendous fun!"

Fun, Masklin thought. It wasn't a familiar word. Perhaps it referred to running through muddy ditches with hungry teeth chasing you. "Do you hunt?" he asked.

"Rats, sometimes. In the Boiler Room. Of course we have to keep them down." He scratched Bobo behind an ear.

"Do you eat them?"

Angalo looked horrified. "Eat *rat*?"

Masklin stared around at the piles of food. "No, I suppose not," he said. "You know, I never realized there were so many nomes in the world. How many live here?"

Angalo told him.

"Two what?" said Masklin.

Angalo repeated it.

"You don't look very impressed," he said when Masklin's expression didn't change.

Masklin looked hard at the end of his spear. It was a piece of flint he'd found in a field one day, and he'd spent ages teasing a bit of binder twine out of a bale of hay in order to tie it on to a stick. Right now it seemed about the one familiar thing in a bewildering world.

"I don't know," he said. "What *is* a thousand?"

Duke Cido de Haberdasheri, who was also Lord Protector of the Up Escalator and Knight of the Counter, turned the Thing over in his hands very slowly. Then he tossed it aside.

"Very amusing," he said.

The nomes stood in a confused group in the Duke's palace, which was currently under the floorboards in the Soft Furnishings Department. The Duke was still in armor, and not very amused.

"So," he said, "and you're from Outside, are you? Do you really expect me to believe you?"

"Father, I—" Angalo began.

"Be quiet! You know the words of Arnold Bros. (est. 1905)! Everything Under One Roof. *Everything!* Therefore, there can be no Outside. Therefore, you people are not from it. Therefore, you're from some under part of the Store. Corsetri. Or Young Fashions, maybe. We've never really explored there."

"No, we're—" Masklin began.

The Duke held up his hands.

"Listen to me," he said, glaring at Angalo. "I don't blame *you*. My son is an impressionable young lad. I have no doubt he talked you into it. He's altogether too fond of going to look at trucks, and he listens to silly stories and his brain gets overheated. Now I am not an unreasonable nome," he added, daring them to disagree, "and there is always room for a strong lad like yourself in the Haberdasheri guards. So let us forget this nonsense, shall we?"

"But we really do come from Outside," Masklin persisted.

"There is no Outside!" said the Duke. "Except of course when a good nome dies, if he has led a proper life. *Then* there is an Outside, where they will live in splendor forever. Come now"—he patted Masklin on the shoulder—"give up this foolish chatter and help us in our valiant task."

"Yes, but what *for?*" said Masklin.

"You wouldn't want the Ironmongri to take our department, would you?" said the Duke. Masklin glanced at Angalo, who shook his head urgently.

"I suppose not," he said, "but you're all nomes, aren't you? And there's masses for everyone. Spending all your time squabbling seems a bit silly."

Out of the corner of his eye he saw Angalo shaking his head desperately.

The Duke went red.

"Silly, did you say?"

Masklin leaned backward to get out of his way, but he'd been brought up to be honest. He felt he wasn't bright enough to get away with lies.

"Well—" he began.

"Have you never heard of honor?" asked the Duke.

Masklin thought for a while, and then shook his head.

"The Ironmongri want to take over the whole Store," said Angalo hurriedly. "That would be a terrible thing. And the Millineri are nearly as bad."

"Why?" said Masklin.

"Why?" said the Duke. "Because they have always been our enemies. And now you may go," he added.

"Where?" said Masklin.

"To the Ironmongri or the Millineri. Or the Stationeri, they're just the people for you. Or go back Outside, for all I care," said the Duke.

"We want the Thing back," said Masklin stolidly. The Duke picked it up and threw it at him.

"Sorry," said Angalo, when they were outside. "I should have told you, Father has rather a temper."

"What did you go and upset him for?" said Grimma irritably. "If we've got to join up with someone, why not with him? What happens to us now?"

"He was very rude," said Granny Morkie stoutly.

"He'd never heard of the Thing," said Torrit. "Terrible, that is. Or Outside. Well, I was borned and bred Outside. Ain't no dead people there. Not living in splendor, anyway."

They started to squabble, which was fairly usual.

Masklin looked at them. Then he looked down at his feet. They were walking a sort of short dry grass that Angalo had said was called *carpet*. Something else stolen from the Store above.

He wanted to say, This is ridiculous. Why is it that as soon as a nome has all he needs to eat and drink, he starts to bicker with other nomes? There must be more to being a nome than this.

And he wanted to say, If humans are so stupid, how is it that they built this Store and all these trucks? If we're that smart, then *they* should be stealing from *us*, not the other way around. They might be big and slow, but they're quite bright, really.

And he wanted to add, I wouldn't be surprised if they're at least as intelligent as rats, say.

But he didn't say any of this, because while he was thinking his eyes fell on the Thing, clasped in Torrit's arms.

He was aware that there was a thought he

ought to be having. He made a space in his head politely and waited patiently to see what it was, and then, just as it was about to arrive, Grimma said to Angalo, "What happens to nomes who aren't in a department?"

"They lead very sad lives," said Angalo. "They just have to get along as best they can."

He looked as if he were about to cry. "*I* believe you," he said. "My father says it's wrong to watch the trucks. They can lead you into wrong thoughts, he says. Well, I've watched them for months. Sometimes they come in wet. It's not all a dream Outside, things happen. Look, why don't you sort of hang around, and I'm sure he'll change his mind."

The Store was big. Masklin had thought the truck was big. The Store was bigger. It went on forever, a maze of floor and walls and long, tiring steps. Nomes hurried or sauntered past them on errands of their own, and there seemed to be no end of them. In fact the word *big* was too small. The Store needed a whole new word.

In a strange way it was even bigger than Outside. Outside was so huge you didn't really see it. It had no edges and no top, so you didn't think of it as having a size at all. It was just *there*. Whereas the Store did have edges and a top, and they were so far away, they were, well, *big*.

As they followed Angalo, Masklin made up his mind and decided to tell Grimma first.

"I'm going back," he said.

She stared at him. "But we've only just arrived! Why on earth . . . ?"

"I don't know. It's all wrong here. It just *feels* wrong. I keep thinking that if I stay here any longer, *I'll* stop believing there's anything Outside, and I was *born* there. When I've got you all settled down I'm going out again. You can come if you like," he added, "but you don't have to."

"But it's warm and there's all this food!"

"I said I couldn't explain. I just feel we're being, well, watched."

Instinctively she stared upward at the underside of the Store floor, a few inches above them. Back home anything watching them usually meant something was thinking about lunch. Then she remembered herself and gave a nervous laugh.

"Don't be silly," she said.

"I just don't feel safe," he said wretchedly.

"You mean you don't feel wanted," said Grimma quietly.

"What?"

"Well, isn't that true? You spend all your time scrimping and scraping for everyone, and then you don't need to anymore. It's a funny feeling, isn't it?"

She swept away.

Masklin stood and fiddled with the binding on

his spear. Odd, he thought. I never thought anyone else would think like that. He had a few dim recollections of Grimma in the hole, always doing laundry or organizing the old women or trying to cook whatever it was he managed to drag home. Odd. Fancy missing something like that.

He began to be aware that the rest of them had stopped. The underfloor stretched away ahead of them, lit dimly by small lights fixed to the wood here and there. Ironmongri charged highly for the lights, Angalo said, and wouldn't let anyone else into the secret of controlling the electricity. It was one of the things that made the Ironmongri so powerful.

"This is the edge of Haberdasheri territory at the moment," he said. "Over there is Millineri country. We're a bit cool with them at the moment. Er. You're bound to find some department to take you in. . . ." He looked at Grimma.

"Er," he said.

"We're going to stay together," said Granny Morkie. She looked hard at Masklin, and then turned back imperiously and waved her hand at Angalo.

"Go away, young man," she said. "Masklin, stand up straight. Now . . . forward."

"Who're you, saying 'forward'?" said Torrit. "I'm the leader, I am. It's my job, givin' orders."

"All right," said Granny Morkie. "Give 'em, then."

Torrit's jaw worked soundlessly. "Right," he managed. "Forward."

Masklin's jaw dropped.

"Where to?" he said as the old woman shooed them along the dim space.

"We will find somewhere. I lived through the Great Winter of 1988, I did," said Granny Morkie haughtily. "The cheek of that silly old Duke man! I nearly spoke up. He wouldn't of lasted long in the Great Winter, I can tell you."

"No 'arm can befall us if we obey the Thing," said Torrit, patting it carefully.

Masklin stopped. He had, he decided, had enough.

"What does the Thing say, then?" he said sharply. "Exactly? What does it actually tell us to do now? Come on, tell me what it says we should do now!"

Torrit looked a bit desperate.

"Er," he muttered, "it, er, is clear that if we pulls together and maintains a proper—"

"You're just making it up as you go along!"

"How dare you speak to him like that—" Grimma snapped.

Masklin flung down his spear.

"Well, I'm fed up with it!" he muttered. "The Thing says this, the Thing says that, the Thing says every blessed thing except anything that might be useful!"

"The Thing has been handed down from nome

to nome for hundreds of years," said Grimma. "It's very important."

"Why?"

Grimma looked at Torrit. He licked his lips.

"It shows us—" he began, white-faced.

"Move me closer to the electricity."

"The Thing seems to be more important than . . . what are you all looking like that for?" said Masklin.

"Closer to the electricity."

Torrit, his hands shaking, looked down at the Thing.

Where there had been smooth black surfaces there were now little dancing lights. Hundreds of them. In fact, Masklin said, feeling slightly proud of knowing what the word meant, there were probably *thousands* of them.

"Who said that?" said Masklin.

The Thing dropped out of Torrit's grasp and landed on the floor, where its lights glittered like a thousand highways at night. The nomes watched it in horror.

"The Thing *does* tell you things . . ." said Masklin. "Gosh!"

Torrit waved his hands frantically. "Not like that! Not like that! It ain't supposed to talk out loud! It ain't done that before!"

"Closer to the electricity!"

"It wants the electricity," said Masklin.

"Well, *I'm* not going to touch it!"

Masklin shrugged and then, using his spear gingerly, pushed the Thing across the floor until it was under the wires.

"How does it speak? It hasn't got a mouth," said Grimma.

The Thing whirred. Colored shapes flickered across its surfaces faster than Masklin's eyes could follow. Most of them were red.

Torrit sank to his knees. "It is angry," he moaned. "We shouldn't have eaten rat, we shouldn't have come here, we shouldn't—"

Masklin also knelt down. He touched the bright areas, gingerly at first, but they weren't hot.

He felt that strange feeling again, of his mind wanting to think certain thoughts without having the right words.

"When the Thing has told you things before," he said slowly, "you know, how we should live proper lives . . ."

Torrit gave him an agonized expression.

"It never has," he said.

"But you said—"

"It *used* to, it *used* to," moaned Torrit. "When old Voozel passed it on to me he said it *used* to, but he said that hundreds and hundreds of years ago it just stopped."

"What?" said Granny Morkie. "All these years, my good man, you've been telling us that the Thing says this and the Thing says that and the Things says goodness knows what."

Now Torrit looked like a very frightened, trapped animal.

"Well?" said the old woman menacingly.

"Ahem," said Torrit. "Er. What old Voozel said was, Think about what the Thing *ought* to say, and then say it. Keep people on the right path, sort of thing. Help them get to the Heavens. Very important, getting to the Heavens. The Thing can help you get there, he said. Most important thing about it."

"*What?*" shouted Granny.

"That's what he told me to do. It worked, didn't it?"

Masklin ignored them. The colored lines moved over the Thing in hypnotic patterns. He felt that he ought to know what they meant. He was certain they meant *something*.

Sometimes, on fine days back in the times when he didn't have to hunt every day, he'd climb farther along the bank until he could look down on the place where the trucks parked. There was a big blue board there, with little shapes and pictures on it. And in the litter baskets the boxes and papers had more shapes and pictures on them; he remembered the long argument they'd had about the chicken boxes with the pictures of the old man with the big whiskers on them. Several nomes had insisted that this was a picture of a chicken, but Masklin had rather felt that humans didn't go around eating old men. There had to be more to it than that. Perhaps old men *made* chicken.

The Thing hummed again.

"Fifteen thousand years have passed," it said.

Masklin looked up at the others.

"You talk to it," Granny ordered Torrit. The old man backed away.

"Not me! Not me! I dunno what to say!" he said.

"Well, *I* ain't!" snapped Granny. "That's the leader's job, is that!"

"Fifteen thousand years have passed," the Thing repeated.

Masklin shrugged. It seemed to be up to him.

"Passed what?" he said.

The Thing gave the impression that it was thinking busily. At last it said, *"Do you still know the meaning of the words* Flight Navigation *and* Recording Computer*?"*

"No," said Masklin earnestly. "None of them."

The light pattern moved.

"Do you know anything about interstellar travel?"

"No."

The box gave Masklin the distinct impression that it was very disappointed in him.

"Do you know you came here from a place far away?" it said.

"Oh, yes. We know that."

"A place farther than the moon."

"Er." Masklin hesitated. The journey had taken

a long time. It was always possible that they had gone past the moon. He had often seen it on the horizon, and he was certain that the truck had gone farther than that.

"Yes," he said. "Probably."

"*Language changes over the years,*" said the Thing thoughtfully.

"Does it?" said Masklin politely.

"*What do you call this planet?*"

"I don't know what *planet* means either," said Masklin.

"*An astronomical body.*"

Masklin looked blank.

"*What is your name for this place?*"

"It's called . . . the Store."

"*Thestore.*" The lights moved, as if the Thing were thinking again.

"Young man, I don't want to stand here all day exchanging nonsense with the Thing," said Granny Morkie. "What we need to do now is sort out where we're going and what we're going to do."

"That's right," said Torrit defiantly.

"*Do you even remember that you are shipwrecked?*"

"I'm Masklin," said Masklin. "I don't know who Shipwrecked is."

The lights changed again. Later, when he got to know the Thing better, Masklin always thought that particular pattern was its way of sighing deeply.

"*My purpose is to serve you and guide you,*" said the Thing.

"See?" said Torrit, who was feeling a bit left out. "We was right about that!"

Masklin prodded the box. "You've been keeping a bit quiet about it lately, then," he said.

The Thing hummed. "*This was to maintain internal power. However, I can now use ambient electricity.*"

"That's nice," said Grimma.

"You mean you sort of drink up the lights?" said Masklin.

"*That will suffice as an explanation for now.*"

"Why didn't you talk before, then?" said Masklin.

"*I was listening.*"

"Oh."

"*And now I await instructions.*"

"In where?" said Grimma.

"I think it wants us to tell it what to do," said Masklin. He sat back on his heels and watched the lights.

"What *can* you do?" he said.

"*I can translate, calculate, triangulate, assimilate, correlate, and extrapolate.*"

"I don't think we want anything like that," said Masklin. "Do we want anything like that?" he asked the others.

Granny Morkie appeared to think about it.

"No," she said eventually, "I don't think we wants any of that stuff. Another banana'd be nice, mind."

"I think all we really want is to go home and be safe," said Masklin.

"Go home."

"That's right."

"And be safe."

"Yes."

Later on those five words became one of the most famous quotations in nome history. They were taught in schools. They were carved in stone. And it's sad, therefore, that at the time no one thought they were particularly important.

All that happened was that the Thing said, *"Computing."*

Then all its lights died, except a small green one, which began to flash.

"Thank goodness for that," said Grimma. "What a horrible voice. What shall we do now?"

"According to that Angalo boy," said Granny, "we have to live very sad lives."

Three

I. For they did not know it, but they had brought with them the Thing, which awoke in the presence of Electricity, and it alone knew their History;

II. For nomes have memories of flesh and blood, while the Thing had a memory of Silicon, which is Stone and perisheth not, whereas the memory of nomes blows away like dust;

III. And they gave it Instructions, *but* knew it not.

IV. It is, they said, a Box with a Funny Voice.

V. But the thing began to Compute the task of keeping all nomes safe.

VI. And the Thing also began to Compute the task of taking all nomes home.

VII. *All* the way Home.

—*From The Book of Nome, Mezzanine v. I–VII*

It was easy to get lost under the floor. It took no effort at all. It was a maze of walls and cables, with drifts of dust away from the paths. In fact, as Torrit said, they weren't exactly lost, more mislaid; there were paths all over the place, between the joists and walls, but no indication of where they led to. Sometimes a nome would hurry past on an errand of his own and pay them no attention.

They dozed in an alcove formed by two huge wooden walls, and woke up in light as dim as ever. There didn't seem to be any night or day in the Store. It did seem noisier, though. There was a distant, all-pervading hubbub.

A few more lights were flashing on the Thing, and it had grown a little cup-shaped, smaller thing that went around and around very slowly.

"Should we look for the Food Hall again?" asked Torrit hopefully.

"I think you have to be a member of a department," said Masklin. "But it can't be the only place with food, can it?"

"It wasn't as noisy as this when we came here," said Granny. "What a din!"

Masklin looked around. There was a space between the woodwork and a distant gleam of very bright light. He edged toward it and stuck his eye to the crack.

"Oh," he said weakly.

"What is it?" Grimma called out.

"It's humans. More humans down there than you've ever seen before."

The crack was where the ceiling joined the wall of a room nearly as big as the truck nest, and it was, indeed, full of humans. The Store had opened.

The nomes had always known that humans lived very slowly. Masklin had almost walked into humans once or twice when he was hunting, and knew that even before one of their huge stupid faces could swivel its eyes he could be off the path and hiding behind a clump of something.

The space below was crowded with them, walking their great slow clumping walk and booming at one another in their vague, deep voices.

The nomes watched, fascinated, for some time.

"What are those things they're holding?" said Grimma. "They look a bit like the Thing."

"Dunno," said Masklin.

"Look, they pick them up, and then give something to the other human, and then it's put in a bag and they go away. They almost look, well, as if they mean what they're doing."

"No, it's like ants," said Torrit authoritatively. "They *seems* intelligent, I'll grant you, but when you looks closely there's nothing really clever about them."

"They build things," said Masklin vaguely.

"So do birds, my lad."

"Yes, but—"

"Humans are a bit like magpies, I've always said. They just want things that glitter."

"Hmm." Masklin decided not to argue. You couldn't argue with old Torrit, unless you were Granny Morkie, of course. He had room for only a certain number of ideas in his head, and once one had taken root, you couldn't budge it. But he wanted to say, If they're so stupid, why isn't it *them* hiding from *us*?

An idea struck him. He lifted up the Thing.

"Thing?" he said.

There was a pause. Then the tinny little voice said, *"Operations on main task suspended. What is it that you require?"*

"Do you know what humans are?" said Masklin.

"Yes. Resuming main task."

Masklin looked blankly at the others.

"Thing?" he said.

"Operations on main task suspended. What is that you require?"

"I asked you to tell me about humans," said Masklin.

"This is not the case. You said, 'Do you know what humans are?' My answer was correct in every respect."

"Well, tell *me* what humans are!"

"Humans are the indigenous inhabitants of the world you now call Thestore. Resuming main task."

"There!" said Torrit, nodding wisely. "I told you, didn't I? They're indigenous. Smart, yes, but basically just indigenous. Just a lot of indigenouses." He hesitated. "Indigenice," he corrected himself.

"Are *we* indigenous?" said Masklin.

"*Main task interrupted. No. Main task resumed.*"

"Course not," said Torrit witheringly. "*We've* got a bit of pride."

Masklin opened his mouth to ask what *indigenous* meant. He knew he didn't know, and he was *certain* that Torrit didn't. And after that he wanted to ask a lot more questions, and before he asked them he'd have to think about the words he used.

I don't know enough words, he thought. Some things you can't think unless you know the right words.

But he didn't get around to it because a voice behind him said, "Powerful strange things, ain't they? And very busy just lately. I wonder what's got into them?"

It was an elderly, rather stocky nome. And drably dressed, which was unusual in the Store. Most of his clothing was a huge apron, its pockets bulging mysteriously.

"Have you been spying on us?" said Granny Morkie.

The stranger gave a shrug.

"I usually come here to watch humans," he

said. "It's a good spot. There isn't usually anyone else here. What department are you?"

"We haven't got one," said Masklin.

"We're just people," said Granny.

"Not indigenous either," Torrit added quickly.

The stranger grinned and slid off the wooden beam he'd been sitting on.

"Fancy that," he said. "You must be these new things I've heard about. *Outsiders?*"

He held out his hand. Masklin looked at it cautiously.

"Yes?" he said politely.

The stranger sighed. "You're supposed to shake it," he said.

"I am? Why?"

"It's traditional. My name's Dorcas del Icatessen." The stranger gave Masklin a lopsided grin. "Do you know yours?" he said.

Masklin ignored this. "What do you mean, you watch humans?" he said.

"I watch humans. Study them, you know. It's a hobby. You can learn a lot about the future by watching humans."

"A bit like the weather, you mean?" said Masklin.

"Weather! Of course, weather!" The nome grinned hugely. "You'd know all about weather. Powerful stuff, weather?"

"You've heard of it?" said Masklin.

"Only the old stories. Hmm." Dorcas looked

him up and down. "I reckoned Outsiders'd have to be a different shape, mind. Life, but not as we know it. You just come along with me. I'll show you what I mean."

Masklin looked slowly around the dusty space between the floors. This was just about it. He'd had just about enough of it. It was too warm and too dry and everyone treated him like a fool and now they thought he was the wrong shape.

"Well—" he began, and under his arm the Thing said, *"We need this person."*

"My word," said Dorcas. "What a tiny radio. They get smaller all the time, don't they?"

Where Dorcas led them was just a hole. Big, square, deep, and dark. A few cables, fatter than a nome, disappeared down into the depths.

"You live down here?" said Grimma.

Dorcas fumbled in the darkness. There was a click. Far above something went bang and there was a distant roaring sound.

"Hmm? Oh, no," he said. "Took me ages to figure this out, did this. It's a sort of floor on a rope. It goes up and down, you know. With humans in it. So I thought, I'm not getting any younger, all those stairs were giving my legs a hard time, so I had a look at the way it worked. Perfectly simple. It'd have to be, o' course, otherwise humans wouldn't know how to use it. Stand back, please."

Something huge and black came down the shaft

and stopped a few inches above their heads. There were clangs and thumps and the now familiar sound of clumsy humans walking about.

There was also, slung under the elevator floor, a small wire basket tied on with pieces of string.

"If you think," said Granny Morkie, "that I'm going to get into a . . . a wire nest on a string, then you've got another—"

"Is it safe?" said Masklin.

"More or less, more or less," said Dorcas, stepping across the gap and fumbling with another little bundle of switches. "Hurry up, please. This way, madam."

"Er, how much more than less?" said Masklin as Granny, astonished at being called madam, got aboard.

"Well, *my* part I'm sure is safe," said Dorcas. "The part above us was put together by humans, though, and you never can tell. Hold tight, please. Going *up!*"

There was a clang above them, and a slight jerk as they began to rise.

"Good, isn't it?" said Dorcas. "Took me ages to bypass all the switches. You'd have thought they'd notice, wouldn't you? They press the button to go down, but if I want to go up, we go up. I used to worry that humans would think it odd that the elevators seemed to go up and down by themselves, but they seem powerful dense. Here we are."

The elevator stopped with another jerk, leaving

the nome's basket level with another underfloor gap.

"Electrical and Domestic Appliances," said Dorcas. "Just a little place I call my own. No one bothers me here, not even the Abbot. I'm the only one who knows how things work, see."

It was a place of wires. They ran under the floor in every direction, great bundles of the things. A few young nomes were taking something to pieces in the middle of it all.

"Radio," said Dorcas. "Amazing thing. Trying to figure out how it talks." He rummaged among piles of thick paper, pulled out a sheet, and sheepishly passed it to Masklin.

It showed a small pinkish cone with a little tuft of hair on top.

The nomes had never seen a limpet. If they had, they'd have known that this drawing looked exactly like one. Except for the hair.

"Very nice," said Masklin uncertainly. "What is it?"

"Umm. It was my idea of what an Outsider would look like, you see," said Dorcas.

"What, with pointy heads?"

"The Rain, you see. In the old legends of the Time before the Store. Rain. Water dropping out of the sky all the time. It'd need to run off. And the sloping sides are so the Wind won't keep knocking it over. I had only the old stories to go on, you see."

"It hasn't even got any eyes!"

Dorcas pointed. "Yes, it has. Tiny ones. Tucked in under the hair so they won't get blinded by the Sun. That's a big bright light in the sky," Dorcas added helpfully.

"We've seen it," said Masklin.

"What's he sayin'?" said Torrit.

"He's saying you ought to of looked like that," said Granny Morkie sarcastically.

"My head ain't that sharp!"

"You're right there, you," said Granny.

"I think you've got it a bit wrong," said Masklin slowly. "It's not like that at all. Hasn't anyone been to *look*?"

"I saw the big door open once," said Dorcas. "The one down in the garage, I mean. But there was just blinding white light Outside."

"I expect it would seem like it, if you spend all your time in this gloom," said Masklin.

Dorcas pulled up an empty cotton reel. "You must tell me about it," he said. "Everything you can remember about the Outside."

In Torrit's lap the Thing began to flash another green light.

One of the young nomes brought some food after a while. And they talked and argued and often contradicted one another while Dorcas listened and asked questions.

He was, he told them, an inventor. Especially of things to do with electricity. Back in the early days, when the nomes first began to tap into the Store's wiring, a good many had been killed. They'd found safer ways to do it now, but it was still a bit of a mystery and there weren't many who were keen to get close to it. That's why the leaders of the big families, and even the Abbot of the Stationeri himself, left him alone. It was always a good idea, he said, to be good at something other people couldn't or didn't want to do. So they put up with his sometimes wondering out loud about the Outside. Provided he wasn't *too* loud.

"I shan't remember it all." He sighed. "What was the other light, the one that you get at Closing Time? Sorry, I mean bite."

"Night," corrected Masklin. "It's called the moon."

"Moon," said Dorcas, rolling the word around his mouth. "But it's not as bright as the Sun? Strange, really. It'd be more sensible to have the brightest light at night, not during the day, when you can see anyway. I suppose you've no idea why, have you?"

"It just happens," said Masklin.

"I'd give anything to see for myself. I used to go and watch the trucks when I was a lad, but I never had the courage to get on one." He leaned closer.

"I reckon," he said, "that Arnold Bros. (est. 1905) put us in the Store to find out things. To learn about it. Otherwise, why have we got brains? What do you think?"

Masklin was rather flattered at being asked, but he was interrupted as soon as he opened his mouth. "People keep talking about Arnold Bros. (est. 1905)," said Grimma. "No one actually says who he is, though."

Dorcas leaned back. "Oh, he created the Store. In 1905, you know. The Bargain Basement, Consumer Accounts, and everything between. I can't deny it. I mean, *someone* must have done it. But I keep telling people, that doesn't mean we shouldn't think about—"

The green light on the Thing went off. Its little spinning cup vanished. It made a faint whirring sound, such as a machine would make to clear its throat.

"*I am monitoring telephonic communications,*" it said.

The nomes looked at one another.

"Well, that's nice," said Grimma. "Isn't that nice, Masklin?"

"*I have urgent information to impart to the leaders of this community. Are you aware that you are living in a constructed entity with a limited life?*"

"Fascinating," said Dorcas. "All those words. You could imagine you could almost understand what it's saying. There's things up there"—he jerked his thumb to the floorboards above them—

"that're just like that. Radios, they're called. With pictures too. Amazing."

"Vitally important I communicate information of utmost significance to community leaders concerning imminent destruction of this artifact," intoned the Thing.

"I'm sorry," said Masklin. "Could you try that again?"

"You do not comprehend?"

"I don't know what *comprehend* means."

"Evidently language has changed in ways I do not understand."

Masklin tried to look helpful.

"I will endeavor to clarify my statement," said the Thing. A few lights flashed.

"Jolly good," said Masklin.

"Big-fella Store him go Bang along plenty soon enough chop-chop?" said the Thing hopefully.

The nomes watched one another's faces. There didn't seem to be any light dawning.

The Thing cleared its throat again. *"Do you know the meaning of the word* destroyed?" it asked.

"Oh, yes," said Dorcas.

"That's what is going to happen to Thestore. In twenty-one days."

Four

I. Woe unto you, Ironmongri and Haberdasheri; woe unto you, Millineri and Del Icatessen; woe unto you, Young Fashions, and unto you, you bandits of Corsetri. And even unto you, Stationeri.

II. For the Store is but a Place inside the Outside.

III. Woe unto you, for Arnold Bros. (est. 1905) has opened the Last Sale. *Everything Must Go.*

IV. But they mocked him and said, You are an Outsider, You don't even Exist.

—*From The Book of Nome, Incoming Merchandise v. I–IV*

Overhead, the humans plodded through their slow and incomprehensible lives. Below, so that the din was muffled by carpet and floorboards into a distant rumbling, the nomes straggled hurriedly along their dusty passageways.

"It couldn't of meant it," said Granny Morkie. "This place is too big. Place as big as this can't be destroyed. Stands to reason."

"I *tole* you, dint I?" panted Torrit, who always cheered up immensely at any news of devastation and terror. "They always said the Thing knows things. And don't you go tellin' me to shut up, you."

"Why do we have to run?" said Masklin. "I mean, twenty-one days is a long time."

"Not in politics," said Dorcas grimly.

"I thought this was the Store?"

Dorcas stopped so suddenly that Granny Morkie cannoned into the back of him.

"Look," he said, with impatient patience, "what do you think nomes should do, eh, if the Store is destroyed?"

"Go Outside," Masklin said.

"But most of them don't even believe the Outside really exists! Even I'm not quite sure about it, and I have an extremely intelligent and questing mind! *There isn't anywhere to go.* Do you understand me?"

"There's masses of Outside—"

"Only if you believe in it!"

"No, it's really there!"

"I'm afraid people are more complicated than you think. But we ought to see the Abbot, anyway.

Dreadful old tyrant, of course, but quite bright in his way. It's just a rather stuffy way." He looked hard at them.

"Possibly best if we don't draw attention to ourselves," he added. "People tend to leave me alone, but it's not a wise thing for people to wander around outside their department without good reason. And since you haven't got a department at all . . ."

He shrugged. He managed, in one shift of his shoulders, to hint at all the unpleasant things that could happen to departmentless wanderers.

It meant using the elevator again. It led into a dusty underfloor area, dimly lit by well-spaced, weak bulbs. No one seemed to be around. After the bustle of the other departments, it was almost unpleasantly quiet. Even quieter, Masklin thought, than the big fields. After all, they were *meant* to be quiet. The underfloor spaces should have nomes in them.

They all sensed it. They drew closer to one another.

"What nice little lights," said Grimma, to break the silence. "Nome size. All different colors, look. And some of them flash on and off."

"We steal boxes of 'em every year, around Christmas Fayre," said Dorcas, without looking around. "Humans put them on trees."

"Why?"

"Search me. To see 'em better, I suppose. You can never tell, with humans," said Dorcas.

"But you know what trees are, then," said Masklin. "I didn't think you'd have them in the Store."

"Of course I know," said Dorcas. "Big green things with plastic prickles on them. Some of 'em are made of tinsel. You can't move for the damn things every Christmas Fayre, I told you."

"The ones we have Outside are huge," Masklin ventured. "And they have these leaves that fall off every year."

Dorcas gave him an odd look.

"What do you mean, 'fall off'?" he said.

"They just curl up and fall off," said Masklin. The other nomes nodded. There were a lot of things lately they weren't certain about, but they were experts on what happened to leaves every year.

"And this happens every year?" said Dorcas.

"Oh, yes."

"Really?" said Dorcas. "Fascinating. And who sticks them back on?"

"No one," said Masklin. "They just turn up again, eventually."

"All by themselves?"

They nodded. When there's one thing you're certain of, you hang on to it. "They seem to," said Masklin. "We've never really found out why. It just happens."

The Store nome scratched his head. "Well, I don't know," he said uncertainly. "It sounds like very sloppy management to me. Are you sure—"

There were suddenly figures surrounding them. One minute dust heaps, the next minute people. The one right in front of the party had a beard, a patch over one eye, and a knife clutched in his teeth. It made his grin so much worse.

"Oh, dear," said Dorcas.

"Who're they?" hissed Masklin.

"Bandits. That's always a problem in Corsetri," said Dorcas, raising his hands.

"What's bandits?" said Masklin blankly.

"What's Corsetri?" said Grimma.

Dorcas pointed a finger at the floorboards overhead. "It's up there," he said. "A department. Only no one's really interested in it because there's nothing in it of any use. It's mainly pink," he added. "Sometimes the elastic—"

"Orr ossessionz orr orr ife," said the head bandit impatiently.

"Pardon?" said Grimma.

"I *edd*, orr ossessionz orr orr ife!"

"I think it's the knife," said Masklin. "I think we'd understand you if you took the knife out."

The bandit glared at them with his one good eye, but took the knife blade out of his mouth.

"I *said*, your possessions or your life!" he repeated.

Masklin gave Dorcas a questioning look. The old nome waved his hands.

"He wants you to give him everything you have," he said. "He won't kill you, of course, but they can be rather unpleasant."

The Outside nomes went into a huddle. This was something beyond their experience. The idea of stealing was a new one to them. Back home there had never been anyone to steal from. If it came to that, there had never been anything to steal.

"Don't they understand plain Nome?" said the bandit.

Dorcas gave him a sheepish grin. "You'll have to excuse them," he said. "They're new here."

Masklin turned around.

"We've decided," he said. "If it's the same to you, we'll keep what we have. Sorry."

He gave Dorcas and the bandit a bright smile.

The bandit returned it. At least he opened his mouth and showed a lot of teeth.

"Er," said Dorcas, "you can't say that, you know. You can't say you don't want to be robbed!" He saw Masklin's look of complete bewilderment. "Robbed," he repeated. "It means having your things taken away from you. You can't just say you don't want it to happen!"

"Why not?" said Grimma.

"Because . . ." The old nome hesitated. "I don't know, really. Tradition, I suppose."

The bandit chief tossed his knife from one hand to the other. "Tell you what I'll do," he said. "You being new and everything. We'll hardly hurt you at all. Get them!"

Two bandits grabbed Granny Morkie.

This turned out to be a mistake. Her bony right hand flashed out and there were two ringing slaps.

"Nerve!" she snapped as the nomes staggered sideways, clutching their ears.

A bandit who tried to hold old Torrit got a pointed elbow in his stomach. One waved a knife at Grimma, who caught his wrist; the knife dropped from his hand and he sank to his knees, making pathetic bubbling noises.

Masklin leaned down, grabbed a handful of the chief's shirt in one hand, and lifted him up to eye level.

"I'm not sure we fully understand this custom," he said. "But nomes shouldn't hurt other nomes, don't you think?"

"Ahahaha," said the chief nervously.

"So I think perhaps it would be a good idea if you went away, don't you?"

He let go. The bandit scrabbled on the floor for his knife, gave Masklin another anxious grin, and ran for it. The rest of the band hurried after him, or at least limped fast.

Masklin turned to Dorcas, who was shaking with laughter.

"Well," he said, "what was that all about?"

Dorcas leaned against a wall for support.

"You really don't know, do you?" he said.

"No," said Masklin patiently. "That's why I asked, you see."

"The Corsetri are bandits. They take things that don't belong to them. They hide out in Corsetri because it's more trouble than it's worth to anyone to drag them out," said Dorcas. "Usually they just try to frighten people. They're really just a bit of a nuisance."

"Why'd that one have his knife in his mouth?" said Grimma.

"It's supposed to make him look tough and devil-may-care, I think."

"I think it makes him look silly," said Grimma flatly.

"He'll feel the back of my hand if he comes back here," said Granny Morkie.

"I don't think they'll be back. I think they were a bit shocked to have people hit them, in fact," said Dorcas. He laughed. "You know, I'm really looking forward to seeing what effect you folks have on the Abbot. I don't think we've ever seen anything like you. You'll be like a . . . a . . . what's that stuff you said there's a lot of Outside?"

"Fresh air?" said Masklin.

"That's right. Fresh air."

And so they came, eventually, to the Stationeri.

•

Go to the Stationeri or to the devil, the Duke had said, meaning that he didn't see a lot of difference between the two. And there was no doubt that the other great families distrusted the Stationeri, who they reckoned had strange and terrifying powers.

After all, they could read and write. Anyone who can tell you what a piece of paper is saying *must* be strange.

They also understood Arnold Bros. (est. 1905)'s messages in the sky.

But it is very hard to meet someone who believes you don't exist.

Masklin had always thought that Torrit looked old, but the Abbot looked so old that he must have been around to give Time itself a bit of a push. He walked with the aid of two sticks, and a couple of younger nomes hovered behind him in case he needed support. His face was a bag of wrinkles, out of which his eyes stared like two sharp black holes.

The tribe clustered up behind Masklin, as they always did now when they were worried.

The Abbot's guest hall was an area walled with cardboard, near one of the elevators. Occasionally one went past, shaking down some dust.

The Abbot was helped to his chair and sat down slowly while his assistants fussed around him. Then he leaned forward.

"Ah," he said, "Del Icatessen, isn't it? Invented anything lately?"

"Not lately, my lord," said Dorcas. "My lord, I have the honor to present to you—"

"I can't see anyone," said the Abbot smoothly.

"Must be blind." Granny sniffed.

"And I can't hear anyone either," said the Abbot.

"Be quiet," Dorcas hissed. "Someone's told him about you! He won't let himself see you! My lord," he said loudly, turning back, "I bring strange news. The Store is going to be demolished!"

It didn't have quite the effect Masklin had expected. The Stationeri priests behind the Abbot sniggered to themselves, and the Abbot permitted himself a faint smile.

"Dear me," he said. "And when is this terrible event likely to occur?"

"In twenty-one days, my lord."

"Well, then," said the Abbot in a kindly voice, "you run along now and, afterward, tell us what it was like."

This time the priests grinned.

"My lord, this is no—"

The Abbot raised a gnarled hand.

"I'm sure you know a great deal about electricity, Dorcas, but you must know that every time there is a Grand Final Sale excitable people say, 'The end of the Store is nigh.' And, strangely enough, life goes on."

Masklin felt the Abbot's gaze on him. For someone who was invisible, he seemed to be attracting considerable attention.

"My lord, it is rather more than that," said Dorcas stiffly.

"Oh? Did the *electricity* tell you?" said the Abbot mockingly.

Dorcas nudged Masklin in the ribs. "Now," he said.

Masklin stepped forward and put the Thing down on the floor.

"Now," he whispered.

"Am I in the presence of community leaders?" said the Thing.

"About as much as you ever will be," said Dorcas.

The Abbot stared at the box.

"I will use small words," said the Thing. *"I am the Flight Recording and Navigation Computer. A computer is a machine that thinks. Think, computer, think. See the computer think. I use elec-tricity. Sometimes elec-tricity can carry messages. I can hear the messages. I can understand the messages. Sometimes the messages go along wires called telephone wires. Sometimes they are in other computers. There is a computer in the Store. It pays humans their wages. I can hear it think. It thinks, No more Store soon, no more payroll, no more accounts. The telephone wires they say, Is that Grimethorpe Demolition Company? Can we discuss final arrangements for the demolition? All stock will be out by the twenty-first—"*

"Very amusing," said the Abbot. "How did you make it?"

"I didn't make it, my lord. These people brought it here—"

"Which people?" said the Abbot, looking straight through Masklin.

"What happens if I go and pull his nose?" whispered Granny in a hoarse whisper.

"It would be extremely painful," said Dorcas.

"Good."

"I mean, for you."

The Abbot rose hesitantly to his feet.

"I am a tolerant nome," he said. "You speculate about things Outside, and I do not mind, I say it is good mental exercise. We wouldn't be nomes if we didn't sometimes allow our minds to wander. But to insist that it is *real*, that is not to be tolerated. Little tricksy toys . . ." He hobbled forward and brought one stick down sharply on the Thing, which buzzed. "Intolerable! There is nothing Outside, and no one to live in it! Life in other stores, pah! Audience concluded! Be off with you."

"*I can stand an impact of 2,500 tons,*" said the Thing smugly, although no one took much notice.

"Away! Away!" shouted the Abbot, and Masklin saw that he was trembling.

That was the strange thing about the Store. Only a few days ago there weren't that many things you needed to know, and they mainly involved big hungry creatures and how to avoid them. Fieldcraft, Torrit had called it. Now it was beginning to dawn on Masklin that there was a different sort of knowledge, and it consisted of the things you needed to understand in order to survive among other nomes. Things like: Be very careful when you tell people things they don't want to hear. And: The thought that they may be wrong makes people very angry.

Some of the lesser Stationeri ushered them hurriedly through the doorway. It was done quite expertly, without any of them actually touching Masklin's people or even looking them in the face. Several of them scattered hastily away from Torrit when he picked up the Thing and held it protectively.

Finally Granny Morkie's temper, which was never particularly long, shortened to the vanishing point. She grabbed the nearest monk by his black robe and held him up inches in front of her nose. His eyes crossed frantically with the effort of not seeing her. She poked him violently in the chest.

"Do you feel my finger?" she demanded. "Do you feel it? Not here, am I?"

"Indigenous!" said Torrit.

The monk solved his immediate problem by giving a little whimper and fainting.

"Let's get away from here," said Dorcas hurriedly. "I suspect it's only a small step between not seeing people and making sure they don't exist."

"I don't understand," said Grimma. "How can people not see us?"

"Because they know we're from Outside," said Masklin.

"But other nomes can see us!" said Grimma, her voice rising. Masklin didn't blame her. He was beginning to feel a bit unsure too.

"I think that's because they don't know," he said, "or don't believe we really *are* Outsiders!"

"I ain't an Outsider!" said Torrit. "They're all Insiders!"

"But that means that the Abbot really does think we're from Outside!" said Grimma. "That means he believes we're here and he can't see us! Where's the sense in that?"

"That's nomish nature for you," said Dorcas.

"Don't see that it matters much," said Granny grimly. "Come three weeks and they'll *all* be Outsiders. Serve them right. They'll have to go around not looking at themselves. See how they like that, eh?" She stuck her nose in the air. "Ho, excuse me, Mr. Abbot, went and tripped over you there, didn't see you I'm sure. . . ."

"I'm sure they'd understand if only they'd listen," said Masklin.

"Shouldn't think so," said Dorcas, kicking at the dust. "Silly of me to think they would, really. The Stationeri never listen to new ideas."

"Excuse me," said a quiet voice behind them.

They turned and saw one of the Stationeri

standing there. He was young and quite plump, with curly hair and a worried expression. In fact, he was nervously twisting the corner of his robe.

"You want me?" said Dorcas.

"Er. I was, er, I wanted to talk to the, er, Outsiders," said the little man carefully. He bobbed a curtsy in the direction of Torrit and Granny Morkie.

"You've got better eyesight than most, then," said Masklin.

"Er, yes," said the Stationeri. He looked back down the corridor. "Er. I'd like to talk to you. Somewhere private."

They shuffled around a floor joist.

"Well?" said Masklin.

"That, er, thing that spoke," said the Stationeri. "Do you believe it?"

"I think it can't actually tell lies," said Masklin.

"What is it, exactly? Some kind of radio?"

Masklin gave Dorcas a hopeful look.

"That's a thing for making noise," Dorcas explained loftily.

"Is it?" said Masklin, and shrugged. "I don't know. We've just had it a long time. It says it came with nomes from a long way away, a long time ago. We've looked after it for generations, haven't we, Torrit?"

The old man nodded violently. "My dad had it before me, and his father before him, and his father before him, and his brother at the same time as him, and their uncle before them . . ." he said.

The Stationeri scratched his head.

"It's very worrying," he said. "The humans are acting very strangely. Things aren't being replaced in the Store. There's signs we've never seen before. Even the Abbot's worried, he can't work out what Arnold Bros. (est. 1905) expects us to do. So, er . . ." He bunched up his robe, untwisted it hurriedly, and went on. "I'm the Abbot's assistant, you see. My name is Gurder. I have to do the things he can't do himself. So, er . . ."

"Well, what?" said Masklin.

"Could you come with me? Please?"

"Is there food?" said Granny Morkie, who could always put her finger on the important points.

"We'll certainly have some sent up," said Gurder hurriedly. He backed off through the maze of joists and wiring. "Please. Follow me. Please."

Five

I. Yet there were some who said, We have seen Arnold Bros. (est. 1905)'s new signs in the Store, and we are troubled, for we Understand them not.

II. For this is the Season that Should Be Christmas Fayre, and yet the signs are not the signs of Christmas Fayre;

III. Nor are they January Sales or Back to School Week or Spring Into Spring Fashions or Summer Bargains, or other signs we know in their season;

IV. For the signs say Clearance Sale. We are Sorely Troubled.

—From The Book of Nome, Complaints v. I–IV

Gurder, bobbing and curtsying, led them deeper into Stationeri territory. It had a musty smell. Here and there was stacks of what Masklin was told were books. He didn't fully understand what they were for, but Dorcas obviously thought they were important.

"Look at 'em," he said. "Powerful lot of stuff in there that we could find useful, and the Stationeri guard it like, like . . ."

"Like something well guarded?" said Masklin.

"Right. Right. That's exactly right. They keep looking hard at 'em. Reading, they call it. But they don't understand any of it."

There was a whir from the Thing in Torrit's arms, and a few lights lit up.

"Books are repositories of knowledge," it said.

"There's said to be a lot in them," said Dorcas.

"It is vital that you obtain books," said the Thing.

"Stationeri holds on to 'em," said Dorcas. "Unless you know how to read books properly they inflame the brain, they say."

"In here, please," said Gurder, shifting a cardboard barrier.

Someone was waiting for them, sitting stiffly on a pile of cushions with his back to them.

"Ah. Gurder," he said. "Come in. Good."

It was the Abbot. He didn't turn around.

Masklin prodded Gurder. "It was bad enough just now," he said. "Why are we doing this again?"

Gurder gave him a look that seemed to say, Trust me, this is the only way.

"Have you arranged for some food, Gurder?" said the Abbot.

"My lord, I was just—"

"Go and do it now."

"Yes, my lord."

Gurder gave Masklin another desperate look and scurried away.

The nomes stood sheepishly, wondering what was going to happen next.

The Abbott spoke.

"I am nearly fifteen years old," he said. "I am older even than some departments in the Store. I have seen many strange things, and soon I am going to meet Arnold Bros. (est. 1905) in the hope that I have been a good and dutiful nome. I am so old that there are nomes who think that in some way I *am* the Store, and fear that when I am gone the Store will end. Now you tell me this is so. Who is in charge?"

Masklin looked at Torrit. But everyone else looked at him.

"Well, er," he said. "Me. I suppose. Just for the moment."

"That's right," said Torrit, relieved. "Just for the moment I'm puttin' him in charge, see. Because I'm the leader."

The Abbott nodded.

"A very wise decision," he said. Torrit beamed.

"Stay here with the talking box," said the Abbot to Masklin. "The rest of you, please go. There will be food brought to you. Please go and wait."

"Um," said Masklin. "No."

There was a pause.

Then the Abbot said, quite softly, "Why not?"

"Because, you see, um, we're all together," said Masklin. "We've never been split up."

"A very commendable sentiment. You'll find, however, that life doesn't work like that. Come, now. I can hardly harm you, can I?"

"You talk to him, Masklin," said Grimma. "We'll only be outside. It's not important."

He nodded reluctantly.

When they had left the Abbot turned around. Close to, he was even older than he had looked before. His face wasn't just wrinkled, it was one big wrinkle. He was middle-aged when old Torrit was born, Masklin told himself. He's old enough to be Granny Morkie's grandfather!

The Abbot smiled. It was a difficult smile. It was as if he'd had smiling explained to him but had never had a chance to practice.

"Your name, I believe, is Masklin," he said.

Masklin couldn't deny it.

"I don't understand!" he said. "You can see me! Ten minutes ago you said I didn't even exist and now you're talking to me!"

"There is nothing strange about it," said the Abbot. "Ten minutes ago it was official. Goodness me, I can't go around letting people believe that I've been wrong all along, can I? The Abbots have been denying there is anything Outside for generations. I can't suddenly say they were all wrong. People would think I've gone mad."

"Would they?" said Masklin.

"Oh, yes. Politics, you see. Abbots can't go changing their minds all the time. You'll find this out. The important thing about being a leader is not being right or wrong but being *certain*. Otherwise people wouldn't know what to think. Of course it helps to be right as well," the Abbot conceded. He leaned back.

"There were terrible wars in the Store once," he said. "Terrible wars. A terrible time. Nome against nome. Decades ago, of course. It seemed that there was always some nome who thought his family should rule the Store. The Battle of the Freight Elevator, the Incoming Merchandise Campaign, the dreadful Mezzanine Wars . . . but that's past now. And do you know why?"

"No," said Masklin.

"*We* stopped it. The Stationeri. By cunning and common sense and diplomacy. We made them see that Arnold Bros. (est. 1905) expects nomes to be at peace with one another. *Now*, then. Supposing that I, in there, had said I believed you. People would have thought, The old boy has gone off his head." The Abbot chuckled. "And then they'd have said, Have the Stationeri been wrong all this time? They would have panicked. Well, of course that would never do. We must hold the nomes together. You know how they bicker at every opportunity."

"That's true," said Masklin. "And they always blame you for everything and say 'What're you going to do about it?'"

"You've noticed, have you?" said the Abbot, smiling. "It seems to me that you have exactly the right qualification for being a leader."

"I don't think so!"

"That's what I mean. You don't want to be one. *I* didn't want to be Abbot." He drummed his fingers on his walking stick, and then looked sharply at Masklin.

"People are always a lot more complicated than you think," he said. "It's very important to remember that."

"I will," said Masklin, not knowing what else to say.

"You don't believe in Arnold Bros. (est. 1905), do you?" said the Abbot. It was more a statement than a question.

"Well, er—"

"I've seen him, you know. When I was a boy. I climbed all the way up to Consumer Accounts, by myself, and hid, and I saw him at his desk, writing."

"Oh?"

"He had a beard."

"Oh."

The Abbot drummed his fingers on his stick. He seemed to be making up his mind about something. Then he said, "Hmm. Where was your home?"

Masklin told him. Funnily, it seemed a lot better now that he looked back on it. More summers than winters, more nuts than rat. No bananas or electricity or carpets, but plenty of fresh air. And in memory there didn't seem to be as much drizzle and frost. The Stationeri listened politely.

"It was a lot better when we had more people," Masklin finished. He glanced at his feet. "You could come and stay. When the Store is demo-thinged."

The Abbot laughed. "I'm not sure I'd fit in," he said. "I'm not sure I want to believe in your *Outside*. It sounds cold and dangerous. Anyway, I shall be going on a rather more mysterious journey. And now, please excuse me, I must rest." He thumped on the floor with his stick. Gurder appeared as if by magic.

"Take Masklin away and educate him a little," said the Abbott. "And then the both of you come back here. But leave that black box, please. I wish to learn more about it. Put it on the floor."

Masklin did so. The Abbot poked it with his stick.

"Black box," he said, "what are you, and what is your purpose?"

"I am the Flight Recorder and Navigation Computer of the starship Swan. *I have many functions. My current major function is to guide and advise those nomes ship-*

wrecked when their scout ship crashed here fifteen thousand years ago."

"It talks like this all the time," said Masklin apologetically.

"Who are these nomes of which you speak?" said the Abbot.

"All nomes."

"Is that your only purpose?"

"I have also been given the task of keeping nomes safe and taking them home."

"Very commendable," said the Abbot. He looked up at the other two.

"Run along, then," he commanded. "Show him a little of the world. And then I shall have a task for both of you."

Educate him a little, the Abbot had said.

That meant starting with The Book of Nome, which consisted of pieces of paper sewn together with marks on them. Nomes had made the marks, Gurder explained. It was called "Righting."

Gurder read them the first dozen verses. They listened in silence, and then Granny Morkie said, "So this Arnold Bros.—"

"—(est. 1905)—" said Gurder primly.

"Whatever," said Granny, "He built the Store just for nomes?"

"Er. Ye-ess," said Gurder uncertainly.

"What was here before, then?" said Granny.

"The Site." Gurder looked uncomfortable.

"You see, the Abbot says there is nothing outside the Store. Um."

"But we've *come*—"

"He says that tales of Outside are just dreams."

"So when I said all that about where we lived, he was just laughing at me?" said Masklin.

"It's often very hard to know what the Abbot really believes," said Gurder. "I think most of all he believes in Abbots."

"*You* believe us, don't you?" said Grimma. Gurder nodded half hesitantly.

"I've often wondered where the trucks go, and where the humans come from," he said. "The Abbot gets very angry when you mention it, though. The other thing is, there's been a new season. That means something. Some of us have been watching humans, and when there's a new season something unusual is happening."

"How can you have seasons when you don't know about weather?" said Masklin.

"Weather has got nothing to do with seasons. Look, someone can take the old people down to the Food Hall, and I'll show you two. It's all very odd. But"—and now Gurder's face was a picture of misery—"Arnold Bros. (est. 1905) wouldn't destroy the Store, would he?"

Six

III. And Arnold Bros. (est. 1905) said, Let
there be Signs, so that All within shall
know the proper running of the Store.
IV. On the Moving Stairs, let the Sign Be:
Dogs and Strollers Must Be Carried;
V. And Arnold Bros. (est. 1905) waxed angry,
for many carried neither dog nor stroller;
VI. On the Elevators, let the Sign Be: This
Elevator to Carry Ten Persons;
VII. And Arnold Bros. (est. 1905) waxed
wroth, for oftimes the Elevators carried
only two or three;
VIII. And Arnold Bros. (est. 1905) said, Truly,
humans *are* stupid, who do not
understand plain language.

—*From The Book of Nome, Regulations v.
III–VIII*

It was a long walk through the busy underfloor world.

They found that Stationeri could go where they liked. The other departments didn't fear them, because the Stationeri weren't a true department. There were no women and children, for one thing.

"So people have to *join?*" said Masklin.

"We are selected," Gurder corrected. "Several intelligent boys from each department every year. But when you're a Stationeri, you have to forget about your department and serve the whole Store."

"Why can't women be Stationeri, then?" said Grimma.

"It's a well-known fact that women can't read," said Gurder. "It's not their fault, of course. Apparently their brains get too hot. With the strain, you know. It's just one of those things."

"Fancy," said Grimma. Masklin glanced sideways at her. He'd heard her use that sweet, innocent tone of voice before. It meant that, pretty soon, there was going to be trouble.

Trouble or not, it was amazing the effect that Gurder had on people. They would stand aside and bow slightly as he went past, and one or two of them held small children up and pointed him out. Even the guards at the border crossings touched their helmets respectfully.

All around them was the bustle of the Store moving through time. Thousands of nomes, Masklin thought. I didn't even think there were any *numbers* that big. A world made up of people.

He remembered hunting alone, running along the deep furrows in the big field behind the highway. There was nothing around but earth and flints, stretching into the distance. The whole sky was an upturned bowl with him at the center.

Here, he felt that if he turned around suddenly he would knock someone over. He wondered what it would be like, living here and never knowing anywhere else. Never being cold, never being wet, never being afraid.

You might start thinking it was never possible to be anything else. . . .

He was vaguely aware that they'd gone up a slope and out through another gap into the big emptiness of the Store itself. It was night—Closing Time—but there were bright lights in the sky, except that he'd have to start learning to call it the ceiling.

"This is the Haberdasheri Department," said Gurder. "Now, do you see the sign hanging up there?"

Masklin peered into the misty distance and nodded. He could see it. It had huge red letter shapes on a white banner.

"It should say Christmas Fayre," said the Stationeri, "That's the right season, it comes after Back to School and before Spring into Spring Fashions. But instead it says"—Gurder narrowed his eyes and his lips moved soundlessly for a moment

—"Final Reductions. We've been wondering what that means."

"This is just a thought," said Grimma sarcastically. "It's only a small idea, you understand. I expect big ideas would make my head explode. But doesn't it mean, well, everything is finally being reduced?"

"Oh, it can't mean anything as simple as that. You have to interpret these signs," said Gurder, "Once they had one saying Fire Sale, and we didn't see them sell any fire."

"What do all the other things say?" said Masklin. Everything being Finally Reduced was too horrible to think about.

"Well, that one over there says Everything Must Go," said Gurder. "But that turns up every year. It's Arnold Bros. (est. 1905)'s way of telling us that we must lead good lives because we all die eventually. And those two over there, they're always there too." He looked solemn. "No one really believes them anymore. There were wars over them years ago. Silly superstition, really. I mean, I don't think there is a monster called Prices Slashed who walks around the Store at night seeking out bad people. It's just something to frighten naughty children with."

Gurder bit his lip. "There's another odd thing," he said. "See those things against the wall? They're called shelves. Sometimes humans take things off them, sometimes they put things on them. But just lately . . . well, they just take things away."

Some of the shelves were empty.

Masklin wasn't too familiar with the subtleties of human behavior. Humans were humans, in the same way that cows were just cows. Obviously there was some way that other cows or humans told them apart, but he'd never been able to spot it. If there was any sense in anything they did, he'd never been able to spot it.

" 'Everything Must Go,' " he said.

"Yes, but not *go*," said Gurder. "Not actually *go*. You don't really think it means actually *go*, do you? I'm sure Arnold Bros. (est. 1905) wouldn't allow it. Would he?"

"Couldn't rightly say," said Masklin. "Never heard of him till we came here."

"Oh, yes," said Gurder in a meek voice. "From Outside, you said. It sounded . . . very interesting. And nice."

Grimma took Masklin's hand and squeezed it gently.

"It's nice here too," she said. He looked surprised.

"Well, it is," she said defiantly. "You know the others think so too. It's warm and there's amazing food, even if they have funny ideas about women's brains." She turned back to Gurder. "Why can't you ask Arnold Bros. (est. 1905) what is going on?"

"Oh, I don't think we should do that!" said Gurder hurriedly.

"Why not? Makes sense if he's in charge," said Masklin. "Have you ever even *seen* Arnold Bros. (est. 1905)?"

"The Abbot did once. When he was young he climbed all the way up to Consumer Accounts. He doesn't talk about it though."

Masklin thought hard about this as they walked back. There had never been any religion or politics back home. The world was just too *big* to worry about things like that. But he had serious doubts about Arnold Bros. (est. 1905). After all, if he had built the Store for nomes, why hadn't he made it nome-sized? But, he thought, it was probably not the time to ask questions like that.

If you thought hard enough, he'd always considered, you could work out everything. The wind, for example. It had always puzzled him until the day he'd realized that it was caused by all the trees waving about.

They found the rest of the group near the Abbot's quarters. Food had been brought up for them. Granny Morkie was explaining to a couple of baffled Stationeri that the pineapples weren't a patch on the ones she used to catch at home.

Torrit looked up from a hunk of bread.

"Everyone's been looking for you two," he said. "The Abbot fellow wants you. This bread's *soft.* You don't have to spit on it like the bread we had at ho—"

"Never you mind going on about that!" snapped Granny, suddenly full of loyalty for the old hole.

"Well, it's true," muttered Torrit. "We never had stuff like this. I mean, all these sausages and meat in big lumps, not stuff you have to kill, no ferreting around in dirty cans . . ."

He saw the others glaring at him and lapsed into shamefaced muttering.

"Shut up, you daft old fool," said Granny.

"Well, we dint have no foxes, I expect?" said Torrit. "Like Mrs. Coom and my old buddy Mert, they never—"

Her furious glare finally worked. His face went white.

"It just wasn't all sunshine," he whispered, shaking his head. "Not all sunshine, that's all I'm saying."

"What does he mean?" said Gurder brightly.

"He don't mean nothing," snapped Granny.

"Oh." Gurder turned to Masklin. "I know what a fox is," he said. "I can read Human books, you know. Quite well. I read a book called"—he hesitated—"*Our Furry Friends*, I think it was. 'A handsome and agile hunter, the red fox scavenges carrion, fruit, and small rodents. It'—I'm sorry, is something wrong?"

Torrit was choking on his bread while the oth-

ers slapped him hurriedly on the back. Masklin
took the young Stationeri by the arm and quickly
walked him away.

"Was it something I said?" said Gurder.

"In a way," said Masklin. "And now I think the
Abbot wants to see us, doesn't he?"

The old man was sitting very still, with the
Thing on his lap, staring at nothing.

He paid them no attention when they came in.
Once or twice his fingers drummed on the Thing's
black surface.

"Sir?" said Gurder, after a while.

"Hmm?"

"You wanted to see us, sir?"

"Ah," said the Abbot vaguely. "Young Gurder,
isn't it?"

"Yes, sir!"

"Oh. Good."

There was silence. Gurder coughed politely.

"You wanted to see us, sir?" he repeated.

"Ah." The Abbot nodded gently. "Oh. Yes.
You, there. The young man with the spear."

"Me?" said Masklin.

"Yes. Have you spoken to this, this thing?"

"The Thing? Well, in a way. It talks funny
though. It's hard to understand."

"It has talked to me. It has told me it was made
by nomes a long time ago. It eats electricity. It says
it can hear electric things. It has said"—he glared

at the Thing in his lap—"it has said that it has heard Arnold Bros. (est. 1905) plans to demolish the Store. It is a mad thing. It talks about stars, it says we came from a star, flying. But . . . there is talk of strange events. I wonder to myself, Is this a messenger from the Management, sent to warn us? Or is it a trap set by Prices Slashed? So!" He thumped the Thing with a wrinkled hand. "We must *ask* Arnold Bros. (est. 1905). We will learn his truth."

"But, sir," Gurder burst out, "you're far too—I mean, it wouldn't be right for you to go all the way to the Top again, it's a terrible, dangerous journey!"

"Quite so, boy. So you will go instead. You can read Human, and your boisterous friend with the spear can go with you."

Gurder sagged to his knees. "Sir? All the way to the Top? But I am not worthy . . ." His voice faded away.

The Abbot nodded. "None of us is," he said. "We are all Shopworn and Final Reductions. Everything Must Go. Now be off, and may Bargains Galore go with you."

"Who's Bargains Galore?" said Masklin, and they went out.

"She's a servant of the Store," said Gurder, who was still trembling. "She's the enemy of the dreadful Prices Slashed, who wanders the corridors at night with his terrible shining light to catch evil nomes!"

"It's a good job you don't believe in him, then," said Masklin.

"Of course I don't," agreed Gurder.

"Your teeth are chattering though."

"That's because my *teeth* believe in him. And so do my knees. And my stomach. It's only my head that doesn't, and it's being carried around by a load of superstitious cowards. Excuse me, I'll go and collect my things. It's very important that we set out at once."

"Why?" said Masklin.

"Because if we wait any longer, I'll be too scared to go."

The Abbot sat back in his chair.

"Tell me again," he said, "about how we came here. You mentioned a color. Mauve, wasn't it?"

"*Marooned,*" said the Thing.

"Ah, yes. From something that flew."

"*A galactic survey ship,*" said the Thing.

"But it got broken, you said."

"*There was a fault in one of the everywhere-engines. It meant we could not return to the main ship. Can it be that this is forgotten? In the early days we managed to communicate with humans, but the different metabolic rates and time sense eventually made this impossible. It was hoped originally that humans could be taught enough science to build us a new ship, but they were too slow. In the end we had to teach them the very basic skills, such as metallurgy, in the hope that they might eventually stop fighting one another long enough to take an interest in space travel."*

"Metal Urgy." The Abbot turned the word over and over. Metal urgy. The urge to use metals. That was humans, all right. He nodded. "What was that other thing you said we taught them? Began with a *G.*"

The Thing appeared to hesitate, but it was learning how to talk to nomes now. *"Agriculture?"* it said.

"That's right. A Griculture. Important, is it?"

"It is the basis of civilization."

"What does that mean?"

"It means yes."

The Abbot sat back while the Thing went on talking. Strange words washed over him, like *planets* and *electronics.* He didn't know what they meant, but they sounded *right.* Nomes had taught humans. Nomes came from a long way away. From a distant star, apparently.

The Abbot didn't find this astonishing. He didn't get about much these days, but he had seen the stars in his youth. Every year, around the season of Christmas Fayre, stars would appear in most of the departments. Big ones, with lots of points and glitter on them, and lots of lights. He'd always been very impressed by them. It was quite fitting that they should have belonged to nomes once. Of course they weren't out all the time, so presumably there was a big storeroom somewhere where the stars were kept.

The Thing seemed to agree with this. The big room was called the Galaxy. It was somewhere above Consumer Accounts.

And then there were these "light-years." The Abbot had seen nearly fifteen years go past, and they had seemed quite heavy at the time—full of problems, swollen with responsibilities. Lighter ones would have been better.

And so he smiled, and nodded, and listened, and fell asleep as the Thing talked and talked and talked. . . .

Seven

"She can't come," said Gurder.

"Why not?" said Masklin.

"Well, it's dangerous."

"So?" Masklin looked at Grimma, who was wearing a defiant expression.

"You shouldn't take girls anywhere dangerous," said Gurder virtuously.

Once again Masklin got the feeling he'd come to recognize often since he'd arrived in the Store. They were talking, their mouths were opening and shutting, every word by itself was perfectly understandable, but when they were all put together they made no sense at all. The best thing to do was ignore them. Back home, if women weren't to go anywhere dangerous, they wouldn't go anywhere.

"I'm coming," said Grimma. "What danger is there, anyway? Only this old Price Slasher and—"

"And Arnold Bros. (est. 1905) himself," said Gurder nervously.

"Well, I'm going to come anyway. People don't need me and there's nothing to do," said Grimma. "What can happen anyway? It's not as if something terrible could happen," she added sarcastically, "like me reading something and my brain over-heating, for example."

"Now, I'm sure I didn't say—" said Gurder weakly.

"I bet the Stationeri don't do their own washing," said Grimma. "Or darn their own socks. I bet—"

"All right, all right," said Gurder, backing away. "But you mustn't lag behind, and you mustn't get in the way. We'll make the decisions, all right?"

He gave Masklin a desperate look.

"You tell her she mustn't get in the way," he said.

"Me?" said Masklin. "I've never told her anything."

The journey was less impressive than he'd expected. The old Abbot had told of staircases that moved, fire in buckets, long empty corridors with nowhere to hide.

But since then, of course, Dorcas had put the elevators in. They only went as far as Kiddies Klothes and Toys, but the Klothians were a friendly people who had adapted well to life on a high floor and always welcomed the rare travelers who came with tales of the world below.

"They don't even come down to use the Food Hall," said Gurder. "They get everything they want from the Staff Rest Room. They live on tea and biscuits, mainly. And yogurt."

"How strange," said Grimma.

"They're very gentle," said Gurder. "Very thoughtful. Very quiet. A little bit *mystical*, though. It must be all that yogurt and tea."

"I don't understand about the fire in buckets, though," said Masklin.

"Er," said Gurder, "we think that the old Abbot might, er, we think his memory . . . after all, he *is* extremely old. . . ."

"You don't have to explain," said Grimma. "Old Torrit can be a bit like that."

"It's just that his mind is not as sharp as it was," said Gurder.

Masklin said nothing. It just seemed to him that if the Abbot's mind was a bit blunt now, it must once have been sharp enough to cut the breeze.

The Klothians gave them a guide to take them

through the outlying regions of the underfloor. There were few nomes this high up. Most of them preferred the busy floors below.

It was almost like being Outside. Faint breezes blew the dust into gray drifts; there was no light except what filtered through from occasional cracks. In the darkest places the guide had to light matches.

He was a very small nome who smiled a lot in a shy way and said nothing at all when Grimma tried to talk to him.

"Where are we going?" asked Masklin, looking back at their deep footprints.

"To the moving stairs," said Gurder.

"Move? How do they move? Bits of the Store move *around*?"

Gurder chuckled patronizingly.

"Of course, all this is new to you. You mustn't worry if you don't understand everything," he said.

"Do they move or don't they?" said Grimma.

"You'll see. It's the only one we use, you know. It's a bit dangerous. You have to be topside, you see. It's not like the elevators."

The little Klothian pointed forward, bowed, and hurried away.

Gurder led them up through a narrow crack in the ancient floorboards into the bright emptiness of a passageway, and there—

—the moving stair.

Masklin watched it hypnotically. Stairs rose out of the floor, squeaking eerily as they did so, and whirred up into the distant heights.

"Wow!" he said. It wasn't much, but it was all that he could think of.

"The Klothians won't go near it," said Gurder. "They think it is haunted by spirits."

"I don't blame them," said Grimma, shivering.

"Oh, it's just superstition," said Gurder. His face was white and there was a tremble in his voice. "There's nothing to be frightened of," he squeaked.

Masklin peered at him.

"Have you ever been here before?" he asked.

"Oh, yes. Millions of times. Often," said Gurder, picking up a fold of his robe and twisting it between his fingers.

"So what do we do now?"

Gurder tried to speak slowly but his voice began to go faster and faster of its own accord: "You know, the Klothians say that Arnold Bros. (est. 1905) waits at the Top, you know, and when nomes die—"

Grimma looked reflectively at the rising stairs and shivered again. Then she ran forward.

"What're you doing?" said Masklin.

"Seeing if they're right!" she snapped. "Otherwise we'll be here all day!"

Masklin ran after her. Gurder gulped, looked behind him, and scurried after both of them.

Masklin saw her run toward the rising bulk of a step, and then the floor below her came up and she was suddenly rising, wobbling as she fought for balance. The floor below him pushed against his feet and he rose after her, one step below.

"Jump down!" he shouted. "You can't trust ground that moves by itself!"

Her pale faced peered over the edge of her step.

"What good will that do?" she said.

"Then we can go and talk about it!"

She laughed. "Go where? Have you looked down lately?"

Masklin looked down.

He was already several steps up. The distant figure of Gurder, his face just a blob, screwed up his courage and jumped onto a step of his own. . . .

Arnold Bros. (est. 1905) was not waiting at the top.

It was simply a long brown corridor lined with doors. There were words painted on some of them.

But Grimma was waiting. Masklin waved a finger at her as he staggered off his step, which mysteriously folded itself down into the floor.

"Never, *ever*, do anything like that again!" he shouted.

"If I hadn't, you'd still be at the bottom. You could see Gurder was scared out of his wits!" she snapped.

"But there could have been all sorts of dangers up here!"

"Like what?" said Grimma haughtily.

"Well, there could be . . ." Masklin hesitated. "That's not the point, the point is—"

At this point Gurder's step rolled him almost to their feet. They picked him up.

"There," said Grimma brightly. "We're all here, and everything's perfectly all right, isn't it?"

Gurder stared around him. Then he coughed and adjusted his clothes.

"I lost my balance there," he said. "Tricky, these moving stairs. But you get used to them eventually." He coughed again and looked along the corridor. "Well, we'd better get a move on," he said.

The three nomes crept forward, past the rows of doors.

"Does one of these belong to Prices Slashed?" said Grimma. Somehow, the name sounded far worse up here.

"Um, no" said Gurder. "He dwells among the furnaces in the Basement." He squinted up at the nearest door. "This one is called Salaries," he said.

"Is that good or bad?" said Grimma, staring at the word on the varnished wood.

"Don't know."

Masklin brought up the rear, turning slowly to keep all the corridor in view. It was too open. There was no cover, nothing to hide behind.

He pointed to a row of giant red things hanging halfway up the opposite wall. Gurder whispered that they were buckets.

"There's pictures of them in *Colin and Susan Go to the Seaside*," he confided.

"What's that written on them?"

Gurder squinted. " 'Fire,' " he said. "Oh, my. The Abbot was right. Buckets of fire!"

"Fire in buckets?" said Masklin. "Buckets of *fire*? I can't see any flames."

"They must be inside. Perhaps there's a lid. There's beans in bean cans, and jam in jam jars. There should be fire in fire buckets," said Gurder vaguely. "Come on."

Grimma stared at this word too. Her lips moved silently as she repeated it to herself. Then she hurried after the other two.

Eventually they reached the end of the corridor. There was another door there, with glass in the top half.

Gurder stared up at it.

"I can see there's words," said Grimma. "Read them out. I'd better not look at them," she added sweetly, "in case my brain goes bang."

Gurder swallowed. "They say 'Arnold Bros. (est. 1905). D. H. K. Butterthwaite, General Manager.' Er."

"He's in there?" she said.

"Well, there's beans in bean cans and fire in fire

buckets," said Masklin helpfully. "The door's not shut, look. Want me to go and see?"

Gurder nodded wretchedly. Masklin walked over to the door, leaned against it, and pushed until his arms ached. Eventually it swung in a little way.

There was no light inside, but by the faint glow from the corridor through the glass top he could see he was entering a large room. The carpet was much thicker—it was like wading through grass. Several yards away was a large rectangular wooden thing; as he walked around it he saw a chair behind it. Perhaps this was where Arnold Bros. (est. 1905) sat.

"Where are you, Arnold Bros. (est. 1905)?" he whispered.

Some minutes later the other two heard him calling softly. They peered around the door.

"Where are you?" hissed Grimma.

"Up here," came Masklin's voice. "This big wooden thing. There's sticking-out parts you can climb on. There's all kinds of things up here. Careful of the carpet, there could be wild animals in it. If you wait a minute, I can help you up."

It took them much longer than that to wade cautiously through the deep pile of the carpet. They waited anxiously by the wooden cliff.

"It's a desk," said Gurder loftily. "There's lots of them in Furnishings. Amazing Value in Genuine 100 Percent Oak Veneer."

"What's he doing up there?" said Grimma. "I can hear clinking noises."

"A Must in Every Home," said Gurder, as if saying the words gave him some comfort. "Wide Choice of Styles to Suit Every Pocket."

"What are you talking about?"

"Sorry. It's the sort of thing Arnold Bros. (est. 1905) writes on the signs. I just feel better for saying it."

"What's that other thing up there?"

He looked where she was pointing.

"That? It's a chair. Swiveled Finish for That Executive Look."

"It looks big enough for humans," she said thoughtfully.

"I expect humans sit there when Arnold Bros. (est. 1905) is giving them their instructions."

"Hmm," she said.

There was a clinking noise by her head.

"Sorry," Masklin called down. "It took me a while to hook them together."

Gurder looked up at the heights and the gleaming chain that now hung down.

"Paper clips," he said, amazed. "I never would have thought it."

When they clambered to the top they found Masklin wandering across the shiny surface, prodding things with his spear. Paper, Gurder explained airily, and things for making marks.

"Well, Arnold Bros. (est. 1905) doesn't seem to

be around," Masklin said. "Perhaps he's gone to bed, or whatever."

"The Abbot said he saw him here one night, sitting at the desk right here," said Gurder. "Watching over the Store."

"What, sitting on that chair?" said Grimma.

"I suppose so. He didn't say."

"So he's big, then, is he?" Grimma pressed on relentlessly. "Sort of human-sized?"

"Sort of," Gurder agreed reluctantly.

"Hmm."

Masklin found a cable as thick as his arm winding off across the top of his desk. He followed it.

"If he's human-shaped and human-sized," said Grimma, "then perhaps he's a—"

"Let's just see what we can find up here, shall we?" said Gurder hurriedly. He walked over to a pile of paper and started reading it by the dim light coming in from the corridor. He read quickly, in a very loud voice.

" 'The Arnco Group' " he read, " 'Incorporating Arnco Developments (U.K.), United Television, Arnco-Schultz (Hamburg) A.G., Arnco Airlines, Arnco Recording, the Arnco Organization (Cinemas), Ltd., Arnco Petroleum Holdings, Arnco Publishing, Arnco U.K. Retailing Plc., and Arnco International Consolidated, Inc."

"Gosh," said Grimma flatly.

"There's more," said Gurder excitedly. "In much smaller letters, perhaps they're meant to be right for *us*. Listen to all these names—'Arnco U.K. Retailing Plc. includes Bonded Outlets, Ltd., the Grimethorpe Dye and Paint Company, Kwik-kleen Mechanical Sweepers, Ltd., and . . . and . . . and . . .' "

"Something wrong?"

" 'Arnold Bros. (est. 1905).' " Gurder looked up. "What do you think it all means? *Bargains Galore preserve us!*"

There was light. It skewered down on the two of them, white and searing, so that they stood over a black pool of their own shadows.

Gurder looked up in terror at the brilliant globe that had appeared above them.

"Sorry, I think that was me," said Masklin's voice from the shadows. "I found this sort of lever thing, and when I pushed it, it went click. Sorry."

"Ahaha," said Gurder mirthlessly. "An electric light. Of course. Ahaha. Gave me quite a start for a moment."

Masklin appeared in the circle of brightness and looked at the paper.

"I heard you reading," he said. "Anything interesting?"

Gurder pored over the print again.

" 'Notice to all Staff' " he read, " 'I am sure we are all aware of the increasingly poor financial performance of the store in recent years. This rambling old building, while quite suitable for the leisured shopper of 1905, is not appropriate in the exciting world of the 1990s, and as we all know, there have unfortunately been marked stock losses and a general loss of custom following the opening of newer major outlets in the city. I am sure our sorrow at the closure of Arnold Bros., which as you know was the foundation of the Arnco fortunes, will be lessened by the news of plans by the Group to replace it with an Arnco Supersaver Store in the Neil Armstrong Shopping Mall. The store will close at the end of the month, and will shortly be demolished to make way for an exciting new Arnco Leisure Complex. . . .' "

Gurder fell silent and put his head in his hands.

"There's those words again," said Masklin slowly. "Closure. Demolished."

"What's leisure?" said Grimma.

The Stationeri ignored her.

Masklin took her gently by the arm.

"I think he wants to be alone for a while," he said. He pulled the tip of his spear across the broad sheet of paper, creasing it, and folded it up until it was small enough to carry.

"I expect the Abbot will want to see it," he said, "He'll never believe us if we—"

He stopped. Grimma was staring over his shoulder. He turned and looked out through the glass part of the great door into the corridor beyond. There was a shadow out there. Human-shaped. And growing bigger.

"What *is* it?" she said.

Masklin gripped the spear. "I think," he said, "it may be Prices Slashed."

They turned and hurried over to Gurder.

"There's someone coming," Masklin whispered. "Get down to the floor, quickly!"

"Demolished!" moaned Gurder, hugging himself and rocking from side to side. "Everything Must Go! Final Reductions! We're all doomed!"

"Yes, but do you think you could go and be doomed on the floor?" said Masklin.

"He's not himself, you can see that," said Grimma. "Come on," she added in a horribly cheerful voice, "upsydaisy."

She lifted him up bodily and helped him toward the rope of clips. Masklin followed them, walking backward with his eye on the door.

He thought, He has seen the light. It should be dark in here now, and he has seen the light. But I'll never get it off in time and, anyway, it won't make any difference. I don't believe in any demon called Prices Slashed, and now here he comes. What a strange world.

He sidled into the shade of a pile of paper and waited.

He could hear Gurder's feeble protests, down around floor level, suddenly stop. Perhaps Grimma had hit him with something. She had a way of taking obvious action in a crisis.

The door drifted open, very slowly. There *was*

a figure there. It looked like a human in a blue suit. Masklin wasn't much of a judge of human expressions, but the man didn't look very happy. In one hand he held a metal tube. Light shone out of one end. His terrible light, Masklin thought.

The figure came closer, in that slow-motion, sleepwalking way that humans had. Masklin peered around the paper, fascinated despite himself. He looked up into a round, red face, felt the breath, saw the peaked hat.

He'd learned that humans in the Store had their names on little badges because—he'd been told—they were so stupid they wouldn't remember them otherwise. This man had his name on his hat, and he was called Security. He had a white mustache.

The man straightened up and started to walk around the room. They're not stupid, Masklin told himself. He's bright enough to know there shouldn't be a light on, and he wants to find out why. He's bound to see the others if he just looks in the right place. Even a human could see them.

He gripped his spear. The eyes, he thought, I'll have to go for the eyes. . . .

Security drifted dreamily around the room, examining cupboards and looking in corners. Then he headed back toward the door.

Masklin dared to breath and, at that moment, Gurder's hysterical voice came from somewhere below him:

"It *is* Prices Slashed! Oh, Bargains Galore, save us! We're all mmphmmphmmph—"

Security stopped. He turned back, a look of puzzlement spreading across his face slowly.

Masklin shrank farther back into the shadows. This is it, then, he thought. If I can get a good run at him . . .

Something outside the door started to roar. It was almost a truck noise. It didn't seem to worry the man, who just pulled the door open and looked out.

There was a human woman in the passage. She looked quite elderly, as far as Masklin was any judge, with a pink apron with flowers on it and carpet slippers on her feet. She held a duster in one hand, and with the other she was . . .

Well, it looked as though she was holding back a sort of roaring thing, like a bag on wheels. It kept rushing forward across the carpet, but she kept one hand on its stick and kept pulling it back.

While Masklin watched she gave the thing a kick. The roaring died away as Security started to talk to her. To Masklin the conversation sounded like a couple of foghorns having a fight.

Masklin ran to the edge of the desk and half climbed, half fell down the chain of clips. The other two were waiting in the shadow of the desk. Gurder's eyes were rolling; Grimma had one hand clamped firmly over his mouth.

"Let's get out of here while he's not looking!" said Masklin.

"How?" said Grimma, "There's only the doorway."

"Mmphmmph."

"Well, let's at least get somewhere better than this." Masklin stared around across the rolling acres of dark carpet. "There's a closet thing over there," he said.

"Mmphmmmph!"

"What are we going to do with *him*?"

"Look," said Masklin to Gurder's frightened face, "you're not going to go on about doom, doom again, are you? Otherwise we'll have to gag you. Sorry."

"Mmph."

"Promise?"

"Mmph."

"Okay, you can take your hand away."

"It was Bargains Galore!" hissed Gurder excitedly.

Grimma looked up at Masklin. "Shall I shut him up again?" she said.

"He can say what he likes as long as he keeps quiet," said Masklin. "It probably makes him feel better. He's had a bit of a shock."

"Bargains Galore came to protect us! With her great roaring Soul Sucker . . ." Gurder's brow wrinkled in puzzlement.

"It was a vacuum cleaner, wasn't it?" he said

slowly, "I always thought it was something magical and it was just a vacuum cleaner. There's lots of them in Household Appliances. With Extra Suction for Deep-Down Carpet Freshness."

"Good. That's nice. Now, how do we get out of here?"

Some searching behind the filing cabinets revealed a crack in the floorboard just big enough to squeeze through with difficulty. Getting back took half a day, partly because Gurder would occasionally sit down and burst into tears, but mainly because they had to climb down inside the wall itself. It was hollow and had wires and sometimes bits of wood in it, tied into place by the Klothians, but it was still a tedious job. They came out under Kiddies Klothes. Gurder had pulled himself together by then and haughtily ordered food and an escort.

And so at last they came back to the Stationeri Department.

Just in time.

Granny Morkie looked up as they were ushered into the Abbot's bedroom. She was sitting by the bed with her hands on her knees.

"Don't make any loud noises," she ordered, "He's very ill. He says he's dyin'. I suppose he should know."

"Dying of what?" said Masklin.

"Dyin' of bein' alive for such a long time," said Granny.

The Abbot lay, wrinkled and even smaller than

Masklin remembered him, among his pillows. He was clutching the Thing in two thin, clawlike hands.

He looked at Masklin and, with a great effort, beckoned him to come closer.

"You'll have to lean over," Granny ordered. "He can't talk above a croak, poor old soul."

The Abbot gently grabbed Masklin's ear and pulled it down to his mouth.

"A sterling woman," he whispered. "Many fine qualities, I am sure. But please send her away before she gives me any more medicine."

Masklin nodded. Granny's remedies, made from simple, honest, and generally nearly poisonous herbs and roots, were amazing things. After one dose of stomachache syrup, you made sure you never complained of a stomachache ever again. In its way it was a sort of cure.

"I can't *send*," he said, "but I can ask."

She went out, shouting instructions, to mix up another batch.

Gurder knelt down by the bed.

"You're not going to die, are you, sir?" he said.

"Of course I am. Everyone is. That's what being alive is all about," whispered the Abbot. "Did you see Arnold Bros. (est. 1905)?"

"Well. Er." Gurder hesitated. "We found some writing, sir. It's true, it says the Store will be demolished. That means the end of everything, sir. Whatever shall we do?"

"You will have to leave," said the Abbot.

Gurder looked horrified.

"But you've always said that everything outside the Store could only be a dream!"

"And you never believed me, boy. And maybe I
was wrong. That young man with the spear, is he
still here? I can't see very well."

Masklin stepped forward.

"Oh, there you are," said the old nome. "This
box of yours."

"Yes?" said Masklin.

"Told me things. Showed me pictures. Store's a
lot bigger than I thought. There's this room they
keep the stars in, not just the glittery ones they
hang from the ceiling at Christmas Fayre, but hundreds of the things. It's called the universe. We
used to live in it, it nearly all belonged to us, it was
our *home*. We didn't live under anyone's floor. I
think Arnold Bros. (est. 1905) is telling us to go
back there."

He reached out and his cold white fingers
gripped Masklin's arm with surprising strength.

"I don't say you're blessed with brains," he
said. "In fact, I reckon you're the stupid but dutiful
kind who gets to be leader when there's no glory in
it. You're the kind who sees things through. Take
them home. Take them all home."

He slumped back onto the pillows and shut his
eyes.

"But—leave the Store, sir?" said Gurder.

"There's thousands of us, old people and babies and everyone, where can we go? There's foxes out there, Masklin says, and wind and hunger and water that drops out of the sky in bits! Sir? Sir?"

Grimma leaned over and felt the old nome's wrist.

"Can he hear me?" said Gurder.

"Maybe," said Grimma. "Perhaps. But he won't be able to answer you because he's dead."

"But he can't die! He's always been here!" said Gurder, aghast. "You've got it wrong. Sir? Sir!"

Masklin took the Thing out of the Abbot's unresisting hands as other Stationeri, hearing Gurder's voice, hurried in.

"Thing?" he said quietly, walking away from the crowd around the bed.

"I hear you."

"Is he dead?"

"I detect no life functions."

"What does that mean?"

"It means yes."

"Oh." Masklin considered this. "I thought you had to be eaten or squashed first. I didn't think you just sort of stopped."

The Thing didn't volunteer any information.

"Any idea what I should do now?" said Masklin. "Gurder was right. They're not going to leave all this warmth and food. I mean, some of the youngsters might, for a lark. But if we're going to survive Outside, we'll need lots of people. Believe me, I know what I'm talking about. And what am I supposed to say to them—Sorry, you've got to leave it all behind?"

The Thing spoke.

"No," it said.

Masklin had never seen a funeral before. Come to that, he'd never seen a nome die from being alive too long. Oh, people had been eaten, or had never come back, but no one had simply come to an end.

"Where do you bury your dead?" Gurder had asked.

"Inside badgers and foxes, often," he'd replied, and hadn't been able to resist adding, "You know. The handsome and agile hunters?"

This was how the nomes said farewell to their dead:

The body of the old Abbot was ceremoniously dressed in a green coat and a pointy red hat. His long white beard was carefully combed out and then he lay, peacefully, on his bed as Gurder read the service.

"Now that it has pleased you, Arnold Bros. (est. 1905), to take our brother to your great Gardening Department beyond Consumer Accounts, where there is Ideal Lawn Edging and an Amazing Floral Display and the pool of eternal life in Easy-to-Lay Polythene with Real Crazy Paving Edging, we will give him the gifts a nome must take on his journey."

The Count de Ironmongri stepped forward. "I give him," he said, laying an object beside the nome, "the Spade of Honest Toil."

"And I," said the Duke de Haberdasheri, "lay beside him the Fishing Rod of Hope."

Other leading nomes brought other things: the Wheelbarrow of Leadership, the Shopping Basket of Life. Dying in the Store was quite complicated, Masklin gathered.

Grimma blew her nose as Gurder completed the service and the body was ceremoniously carried away.

To the Subbasement, they later learned, and the incinerator. Down in the realms of Prices Slashed, the Security, where he sat at nighttimes, legend said, and drank his horrible tea.

"That's a bit dreadful, I reckon," said Granny Morkie as they stood around aimlessly afterward. "In my young day, if a person died, we buried 'em. In the ground."

"Ground?" said Gurder.

"Sort of floor," explained Granny.

"Then what happened?" said Gurder.

Granny looked blank. "What?" she said.

"Where did they go after that?" said the Stationeri patiently.

"Go? I don't reckon they went anywhere. Dead people don't get about much."

"In the Store," said Gurder slowly, as if he were explaining things to a rather backward child, "when a nome dies, if he has been a *good* nome, Arnold Bros. (est. 1905) sends them back to see us before they go to a Better Place."

"How can—" Granny began.

"The inner bit of them, I mean," said Gurder, "the bit inside you that's really you."

They looked at him politely, waiting for him to make any sort of sense.

Gurder sighed. "All right," he said. "I'll get someone to show you."

They were taken to the Gardening Department. It was a strange place, Masklin thought. It was like the world outside but with all the difficult parts taken away. The only illumination was the faint glow of the lights, which stayed on all night. There was no wind, no rain, and there never would be. There was grass, but it was just painted green sacking with bits sticking out of it. There were mountainous cliffs of nothing but seeds in packets, each one with a picture that Masklin suspected was quite unreal. They showed flowers, but flowers unlike any he'd ever seen before.

"Is the Outside like this?" said the young priest who was guiding them. "They say, they say, er, they say you've been there. They say you've *seen* it." He sounded hopeful.

"There was more green and brown," said Masklin flatly.

"And flowers?" said the priest.

"*Some* flowers," Masklin agreed. "But not like these."

"I seed flowers like these once," said Torrit, and then, unusual for him, he fell silent.

They were led around the bulk of a giant lawn mower and there—

—were nomes. Tall, chubby-faced nomes. Pink-cheeked painted nomes. Some of them held fishing rods or spades. Some of them were pushing painted wheelbarrows. And every single one of them was grinning.

The tribe stood in silence for some time.

Then Grimma said, very softly, "How horrible."

"Oh, no!" said the priest, horrified, "It's marvelous! Arnold Bros. (est. 1905) sends you back smart and new, and then you leave the Store and go to a wonderful place!"

"There's no women," said Granny. "That's a mercy, anyway."

"Ah, well," said the priest, looking a bit embarrassed, "that's always been a bit of a debatable question, we're not sure why but we think—"

"And they don't look like anyone," said Granny. "They all look the same."

"Well, you see—"

"Catch me coming back like that," said

Granny. "If you come back like that, I don't want to go."

The priest was almost in tears.

"No, but—"

"I saw one like these oncet." It was old Torrit again. He looked very gray in the face and was trembling.

"You shut up, you," said Granny. "You never saw nothing."

"I did too," said Torrit. "When I was little lad. Grandpa Dimpo took some of us right across the fields, right through the wood, and there was all these big stone houses where humans lived and they had little fields in front full of flowers like what they got here, and grass all short, and ponds with orange fish, and we saw one of these. It was sitting on a stone toadstool by one of these ponds."

"It never was," said Granny automatically.

"It was an' all," said Torrit levelly. "And I mind Grandpa sayin', 'That ain't no life, out there in all weathers, birds doing their wossname on your hat and dogs widdlin' all over you.' He tole us it was a giant nome who got turned to stone on account of sitting there for so long and never catching no fish. And he said, 'Wot a way to go, that ain't for me, lads, I want to go sudden like,' and then a cat jumped out on him. Talk about laugh."

"What happened?" said Masklin.

"Oh, we gave it a good seeing-to with our

spears and picked him up and we all run like he—
run very fast," said Torrit, watching Granny's
stern expression.

"No, no!" wailed the priest, "it's not like that at
all!" And then he started to sob.

Granny hesitated for a moment, and then patted him gently on the back.

"There, there," she said. "Don't you worry
about it. Daft old fool says any old thing that
comes into his head."

"I don't—" Torrit began. Granny's warning
look stopped him.

They went back slowly, trying to put the terrible stone images out of their minds. Torrit trailed
along behind, grumbling like a worn-out thunder-
storm.

"I did see it, I'm telling you," he whispered.
"Great grinning thing it were, sitting on a spotty
stone mushroom. I did see it. Never went back
there though. Better safe than sorry, I always said.
But I did see it."

It seemed taken for granted by everyone
that Gurder was going to be the new Abbot. The
old Abbot had left strict instructions. There didn't
seem to be any argument.

The only one against the idea, in fact, was
Gurder.

"Why me?" he said. "I never wanted to lead
anyone! Anyway . . . you know"—he lowered his

voice—"I have doubts, sometimes. The old Abbot knew it, I'm sure. I can't imagine why he'd think I'd be any good."

Masklin said nothing. It occurred to him that the Abbot might have had a very definite aim in mind. Perhaps it was time for a little doubt. Perhaps it was time to look at Arnold Bros. (est. 1905) in a different way.

They were off to one side in the big underfloor area the Stationeri used for important meetings; it was the one place in the Store, apart from the Food Hall, where fighting was strictly forbidden. The heads of the families, rulers of departments and subdepartments, were milling around out here. They might not be allowed to bear weapons, but they were cutting one another dead at every opportunity.

Getting them to even think of working together would be impossible without the Stationeri. It was odd, really. The Stationeri had no real power at all, but all the families needed them and none of them feared them and so they survived and, in a strange sort of way, led. A Haberdasheri wouldn't listen even to common sense from an Ironmongri, just on general principles, but he would if the speaker was a Stationeri, because everyone knew the Stationeri didn't take sides.

He turned to Gurder.

"We need to talk to someone in the Ironmongri.

They control the electricity, don't they? And the truck nest."

"That's the Count de Ironmongri over there," said Gurder, pointing. "Thin fellow with the mustache. Not very religious. Doesn't know much about electricity, though."

"I thought you told me—"

"Oh, the *Ironmongri* do. The underlings and servants and whatnot. But not people like the Count. Good heavens"—Gurder smiled—"you don't think the Duke de Haberdasheri ever touches a pair of scissors, do you, or Lady del Icatessen goes and cuts up food her actual self?"

He looked sideways at Masklin.

"You've got a plan, haven't you?" he said.

"Yes. Sort of."

"What are you going to tell them, then?"

Masklin picked absently at the tip of his spear.

"The truth. I'm going to tell them they can leave the Store and take it all with them. I think it should be possible."

Gurder rubbed his chin. "Hmm," he said. "I *suppose* it's possible. If everyone carries as much food and stuff as they can. But it'll soon run out and, anyway, you can't carry electricity. It lives in wires, you know."

"How many Stationeri can read Human?" said Masklin, ignoring him.

"All of us can read a bit, of course," said

Gurder. "But only four of us are any real good at it, if you must know."

"I don't think that's going to be enough," said Masklin.

"Well, there's a trick to it, and not everyone can get the hang of it. What *are* you planning?"

"A way to get everyone, *everyone*, out. Carrying everything we'll ever need, ever," said Masklin.

"They'll be squashed under the weight!"

"Not really. Most of what they'll be carrying doesn't weigh anything at all."

Gurder looked worried.

"This isn't some mad scheme of Dorcas's, is it?" he said.

"No."

Masklin felt that he might explode. His head wasn't big enough to hold all the things the Thing had told him.

And he was the only one. Oh, the Abbot had known, and died with his eyes full of stars, but even he hadn't understood. The Galaxy! The old man thought it was just a great big room outside the Store, just the biggest department ever. Perhaps Gurder wouldn't comprehend, either. He'd lived all his life under a roof. He had no idea of the sort of distances involved.

Masklin felt a slight surge of pride at this. The Store nomes *couldn't* understand what the Thing was saying, because they had no experiences to draw on. To them, from one end of the Store to the other was the biggest possible distance in the world.

They wouldn't be able to come to grips with the fact that the stars, for instance, were much farther away. Even if you ran all the way, it'd probably take *weeks* to reach them.

He'd have to lead up to it gently.

The stars! And a long, long time ago nomes had traveled among them on things that made trucks look tiny—and had been built by nomes. And one of the great ships, exploring around a little star on the edge of nowhere, had sent out a smaller ship to land on the world of the humans.

But something had gone wrong. Masklin hadn't understood that bit, except that the force that moved the ships was very, very powerful. Hundreds of nomes had survived, though. One of them, searching through the wreckage, had found the Thing. It wasn't any good without electricity to eat, but the nomes had kept it, nevertheless, because it had been the machine that steered the ship.

And the generations had passed by, and the nomes forgot everything except that the Thing was very important.

That was enough for one head to carry, Masklin thought. But it wasn't the most important part, it wasn't the part that made his blood fizz and his fingers tingle.

This was the important part. The big ship, the one that could fly among stars, was still up there somewhere. It was tended by machines like the Thing, patiently waiting for the nomes to come back. Time meant nothing to them. There were machines to sweep the long corridors, and machines that made food and watched the stars and patiently counted the hours and minutes in the long, dark emptiness of the ship.

And they'd wait forever. They didn't know what Time was, except something to be counted and filed away. They'd wait until the sun went cold and the moon died, carefully repairing the ship and keeping it ready for the nomes to come back.

To take them Home.

And while they waited, Masklin thought, we forgot all about them, we forgot everything about ourselves, and lived in holes in the ground.

He knew what he had to do. It was, of course, an impossible task. But he was used to them. Dragging a rat all the way from the wood to the hole had been an impossible task. But it wasn't impossible to drag it a little way, so you did that, and then you had a rest, and then you dragged it a little way again. . . . The way to deal with an impossible task was to chop it down into a number of merely very difficult tasks, and break each one of *them* into a group of horribly hard tasks, and each of *them* into tricky jobs, and each one of them . . .

Probably the hardest job of all was to make

nomes understand what they once were and could be again.

He did have a plan. Well, it had started off as the Thing's plan, but he'd turned it over and over in his mind so much he felt it belonged to him. It was probably an impossible plan. But he'd never know unless he tried it.

Gurder was still watching him cautiously.

"Er," Masklin said. "This plan . . ."

"Yes?" said Gurder.

"The Abbot told me that the Stationeri have always tried to make nomes work together and stop squabbling," said Masklin.

"That has always been our desire, yes."

"*This* plan will mean they'll *have* to work together."

"Good."

"Only I don't think you're going to like it much," said Masklin.

"That's unfair! How can you make assumptions like that?"

"I think you'll laugh at it," said Masklin.

"The only way to find out is to tell me," said Gurder.

Masklin told him. When Gurder was over the shock, he laughed and laughed.

And then he looked at Masklin's face and stopped.

"You're not serious?" he said.

"Let me put it like this," said Masklin. "Have you got a better plan? Will you support me?"

"But how will you—how can nomes—is it even possible that we can—" Gurder began.

"We'll find a way," said Masklin. "With Arnold Bros. (est. 1905)'s help, of course," he added diplomatically.

"Oh. Of course," said Gurder weakly. He pulled himself together.

"Anyway, if I'm to be the new Abbot I have to make a speech," he said. "It's expected. General messages of goodwill and so on. We can talk about this later. Reflect upon it at leisure in the sober surroundings of—"

Masklin shook his head. Gurder swallowed.

"You mean *now*?" he said.

"Yes. Now. We tell them *now*."

Eight

I. And the leaders of the nomes were assembled, and the Abbot Gurder said unto them, Harken to the words of the Outsider.

II. And some waxed wroth, saying, He *is* an Outsider, whereforthen shall we harken to him?

III. The Abbot Gurder said, Because the old Abbot wished it so. Yea, and because I wish it so, also.

IV. Whereupon they grumbled, but were silent.

V. The Outsider said, Concerning the Rumors of Demolition, I have a Plan.

VI. Let us not go like wood lice fleeing from an overturned log, but like brave free people, at a time of our choosing.

VII. And they interrupted him, saying, What's wood lice? Whereupon the Outsider said, All right, rats.

VIII. Let us take with us the things that we
      need to begin our life anew Outside, not
      in some other store, but under the sky.
      Let us take all nomes, the aged and the
      young, and all the food and materials and
      information that we need.
  IX. And they said, All? And he said, All. And
      they said unto him, We cannot do this
      thing. . . .

*—From The Book of Nome, Third Floor
v. I–IX*

"Yes, we can," said Masklin, "if we steal a truck."

There was a dead silence.

The Count de Ironmongri raised an eyebrow.

"The big smelly things with wheels at each corner?" he said.

"Yes," said Masklin. All eyes were on him. He felt himself beginning to blush.

"The nome's a fool!" snapped the Duke de Haberdasheri. "Even if the Store were in danger, and I see no reason, no reason I say, to believe it, the idea is quite preposterous."

"You see," said Masklin, "there's plenty of room, we can take everyone, we can steal books that tell us how to do things—"

"The mouth moves, the tongue waggles, but no sense comes out," said the Duke. There was nervous laughter from some of the nomes around him. Out of the corner of his eye Masklin saw Angalo standing by his father, his face shining.

"No offense to the late Abbot," said one of the lesser lords hesitantly, "but I've heard there are other stores Out There. I mean to say, we must have lived somewhere before the Store." He swallowed. "What I'm getting at, if the Store was built in 1905, where did we live in 1904? No offense meant."

"I'm not talking about going to another store," said Masklin. "I'm talking about living free."

"And I'm listening to no more of this nonsense. The old Abbot was a sound man, but he must have gone a little funny in the head at the finish," snapped the Duke. He turned and stormed out noisily. Most of the other lords followed him. Some of them quite reluctantly, Masklin noticed; if fact, a few hung around at the back, so that if asked they could say that they were just about to leave.

Those left were the Count, a small fat woman, whom Gurder had identified as the Baroness del Icatessen, and a handful of lesser lords from the subdepartments.

The Count looked around theatrically.

"Ah," he said. "Room to breathe. Carry on, young man."

"Well, that's about it," Masklin admitted. "I can't plan anything more until I've found out more things. For example, can you make electricity? Not steal it from the Store, but make it?"

The Count stroked his chin.

"You are asking me to give you departmental secrets?" he said.

"My lord," said Gurder sharply, "if we take this desperate step, it is vital that we be open with one another and share our knowledge."

"That's true," said Masklin.

"Quite," said Gurder sternly. "We must all act for the good of all nomes."

"Well said," said Masklin. "And that's why the Stationeri, for their part, will teach all nomes who request it—to read."

There was a pause. It was broken by the faint wheezing noise of Gurder trying not to choke.

"To read . . . !" he began.

Masklin hesitated. Well, he'd gone this far. Might as well get it over with. He saw Grimma staring at him.

"Women too," he said.

This time it was the Count who looked surprised. The Baroness, on the other hand, was smiling. Gurder was still making little mewling noises.

"There's all kinds of books on the shelves in the Stationeri Department," Masklin plunged on. "Anything we want to do, there's a book that tells us how! But we're going to need lots of people to read them so we can find out what we need."

"I think our Stationeri friend would like a

drink of water," observed the Count. "I think he may be overcome by the new spirit of sharing and cooperation."

"Young man," said the Baroness, "what you say might be true, but do these precious books tell us how one may control one of these truck things?"

Masklin nodded. He had been ready for this one. Grimma came up behind him, dragging a thin book that was nearly as big as she was. Masklin helped her prop it up so they could all see it.

"See, it's got words on it," he said proudly. "I've learned them already. They say"—he pointed each one out with his spear as he said them—"the . . . High . . . Way . . . Code. High Way Code. It's got pictures inside. When you learn the High Way Code you can drive. It says so. High Way Code," he added uncertainly.

"And I've been working out what some of the words mean," said Grimma.

"And she's been reading some of the words," Masklin agreed. He couldn't help noticing that this fact interested the Baroness.

"And that is all there is to it?" said the Count.

"Er," said Masklin. He'd been worrying about this himself. He had an obscure feeling that it couldn't be as easy as that, but this was no time to worry about details that could be dealt with later. What was it the Abbot had said? The important thing about being a leader was not so much being right or wrong as being certain. Being right helped, of course.

"Well, I went and looked in the truck nest. I mean the garage, this morning," he said. "You can see inside them if you climb up. There's levers and wheels and things, but I suppose we can find out what they do." He took a deep breath. "It can't be very difficult, otherwise humans wouldn't be able to do it."

The nomes had to concede this.

"Most intriguing," said the Count. "May I ask what it is you require from us now?"

"People," said Masklin simply. "As many as you can spare. *Especially* the ones you can't spare. And they'll need to be fed."

The Baroness glanced at the Count. He nodded, so she nodded.

"I'd just like to ask the young lady," she said, "whether she feels all right. With this reading, I mean."

"I can only do some words," said Grimma quickly. "Like *left* and *right* and *bicycle.*"

"And you haven't experienced any feelings of pressure in the head?" said the Baroness carefully.

"Not really, ma'am."

"Hmm. That's extremely interesting," said the Baroness, staring fixedly at Gurder.

The new Abbot was sitting down now. "I . . . I . . ." he began.

Masklin groaned inwardly. He'd thought it

would be difficult, learning to drive, learning how
a truck worked, learning to *read*, but they were,
well, just tasks. You could see all the difficulties
before you started. If you worked at them for long
enough, then you were bound to succeed. He'd
been right. The difficult thing was going to be all
the people.

There turned out to be twenty-eight.
"Not enough," said Grimma.
"It's a start," said Masklin. "I think there will
be more by and by. They all need to be taught to
read. Not well, but enough. And then five of the
best of them must be taught how to teach people to
read."
"How did you work that out?" said Grimma.
"The Thing told me," said Masklin. "It's some-
thing called Critical Path Analysis. It means
there's always something you should have done
first. For example, if you want to build a house,
you need to know how to make bricks, and before
you can make bricks you need to know what kind
of clay to use. And so on."
"What's clay?"
"Don't know."
"What're bricks?"
"Not sure."
"Well, what's a house?" she demanded.
"Haven't quite worked it out," said Masklin.
"But anyway, it's all very important. Critical Path

Analysis. And there's something else called Progress Chasing."

"What's *that*?"

"I think it means shouting at people 'Why haven't you done it yet?' " Masklin looked down at his feet. "I think we can get Granny Morkie to do that," he said. "I don't reckon she will be interested in learning to read, but she knows how to shout."

"What about me?"

"I want you to learn to read even more."

"Why?"

"Because we need to learn how to think," said Masklin.

"I know how to think!"

"Dunno," said Masklin. "I mean, yes, you do, but there's some things we can't think because we don't know the words. Like the Store nomes. They don't even know what the wind and rain are really like!"

"I know, and I tried to tell the Baroness about snow and—"

Masklin nodded. "There you are, then. They don't know, and they don't even *know* they don't know. What is it that *we* don't know? We ought to read everything we can. Gurder doesn't like it. He says only Stationeri should read. But the trouble is, they don't try to understand things."

Gurder had been furious.

"*Reading*," he'd said. "Every stupid nome coming up here and wearing all the printing out with looking at it! Why don't you give away all our skills while you're about it? Why don't we teach everyone to write, eh?"

"We can do that later," said Masklin mildly.

"What!"

"It isn't so important, you see."

Gurder thumped the wall. "Why in the name of Arnold Bros. (est. 1905) didn't you ask my permission first?"

"Would you have given it?"

"No!"

"That's why, you see," said Masklin.

"When I said I'd help you I didn't expect this!" shouted Gurder.

"Nor did I!" snapped Masklin.

The new Abbot paused.

"What do you mean?" he said.

"I thought you'd help," said Masklin simply.

Gurder sagged. "All right, all right," he said. "You know I can't forbid it now, not in front of everyone. Do whatever is necessary. Take whatever people you must."

"Good," said Masklin. "When can you start?"

"Me? But—"

"You said yourself that you're the best reader."

"Well, yes, of course, this is the case, but—"

"Good."

They grew used to that word, later. Masklin developed a way of saying it that indicated that everything was all settled and there was no point in anyone saying anything more.

Gurder waved his hands wildly.

"What do you want me to do?" he said.

"How many books are there?" said Masklin.

"Hundreds! Thousands!"

"Do you know what they're all about?"

Gurder looked at him blankly. "Do you know what you're saying?" he said.

"No. But I want to find out."

"They're about everything! You'd never believe it! They're full of words even I don't understand!"

"Can you find a book that tells you how to understand words you don't understand?" said Masklin. This is Critical Path Analysis, he thought. Gosh, I'm doing it without thinking.

Gurder hesitated. "It's an intriguing thought," he said.

"I want to find out everything about trucks and electricity and food," said Masklin. "And then I want you to find a book about, about . . ."

"Well?"

Masklin looked desperate. "Is there a book that tells you how nomes can drive a truck built for humans?" he said.

"Don't you know?"

"Not . . . exactly. I was sort of hoping we could work it out as we went along."

"But you said all we needed to do was learn the High Way Code!"

"Ye-ss," said Masklin uncertainly, "and it *says* you have to know the High Way Code before you can drive. But somehow I get the feeling that it might not be as simple as that."

"Bargains Galore, preserve us!"

"I hope so," said Masklin. "I really do."

And then it was time to put it all to the test:

It was cold in the truck nest and stank of *all*. It was also a long way to the ground if they fell off the girder. Masklin tried not to look down.

There was a truck below them. It looked much bigger indoors. Huge, red, and terrible in the gloom.

"This is about far enough," he said. "We're right over the sticking-out part where the driver sits."

"The cab," said Angalo.

"Right. The cab."

Angalo had been a surprise. He'd turned up in the Stationeri Department breathing heavily, his face red, and demanding to be taught to read.

So he could learn about trucks.

They fascinated him.

"But your father objects to the whole idea," Masklin had said.

"That doesn't matter," said Angalo shortly. "It's all right for you, you've *been* there! I want to see all those things, I want to go Outside, I want to know if it's real!"

He hadn't been very good at reading, but he'd tried until his brain hurt when the Stationeri found him some books with trucks on the front. Now he probably knew more about them than any other nome. Which wasn't a lot, Masklin had to admit.

He listened to Angalo muttering to himself as he struggled into the straps.

"Gear," he said. "Shift. Steering Wheel. Wipers. Auto Transmission. Breaker Break Good Buddy. Smokey. Double Egg and Ham and Hash Browns. Truckers." He looked up and smiled thinly at Masklin. "Ready," he said.

"Now remember," said Masklin, "they don't always leave the windows open, so if they're closed, one pull on the rope and we'll pull you back up, okay?"

"Ten-four."

"What?"

"It's truck driver for *yes,*" explained Angalo.

"Oh. Fine. Now, when you're in, find somewhere to hide so you can watch the driver—"

"Yes, yes. You explained it all before," said Angalo impatiently.

"Yes. Well. Have you got your sandwiches?" Angalo patted the package at his waist. "And my notebook," he said. "Ready to go. Put the pedal to the metal."

"What?"

"It means *go* in Truck."

Masklin looked puzzled. "Do we have to know all this to drive one?"

"Negatory," said Angalo proudly.

"Oh? Well, as long as you understand yourself, that's the main thing." Dorcas, who was in charge of the rope detail, tapped Angalo on the shoulder.

"You sure you won't take the Outside suit?" he said hopefully.

It was cone-shaped, made of heavy cloth over a sort of umbrella frame of sticks so that it folded up, and it had a little window to look out of. Dorcas had insisted on building it to protect Outsidegoers.

"After all," he'd said to Masklin, "*you* might be used to the Rain and the Wind, perhaps your heads have grown especially hard. Can't be too careful."

"I don't think so, thank you," said Angalo politely. "It's so heavy, and I don't expect I'll go outside the truck this trip."

"Good," said Masklin. "Well, let's not hang about. Except for you, Angalo. Haha. Ready to take the strain, lads? Over you go, Angalo," he said, and then, because it paid to be on the safe side and you never knew, it might help, he added, "May Arnold Bros. (est. 1905) watch over you."

Angalo eased himself over the edge and slowly became a small spinning shape in the gloom as the team carefully let the thread out. Masklin prayed that they'd brought enough of it, there hadn't been time to come and measure.

There was a desperate tugging on the thread.

Masklin peered down. Angalo was a small shape several feet below him.

"If anything should happen to me, no one is to eat Bobo," he called up.

"Don't you worry," said Masklin. "You're going to be all right."

"Yes, I know. But if I'm not, Bobo is to go to a good home," said Angalo.

"Right you are. A good home. Yes."

"Where they don't eat rat. Promise?"

"No rat eating. Fine," said Masklin.

Angalo nodded. The gang started to pay out the thread again.

Then the boy was down and hurrying across the sloping roof to the side of the cab. It made Masklin dizzy just to look down at him.

The figure disappeared. After a while came two tugs, meaning "pay out more thread." They let it slip past by inches. And then there were three tugs, faint but—well, three. And in a few seconds they came again.

Masklin let out his breath in a whoosh.

"Angalo has landed," he said. "Pull the thread back up. We'll leave it here, in case—I mean, for when he comes back."

He risked another look at the forbidding bulk of the truck. The trucks went out, the trucks came back, and it was the considered opinion of nomes like Dorcas that they were the same trucks. They went out loaded with goods, and they came back loaded with goods, and why Arnold Bros. (est. 1905) felt the need to let goods out for the day was beyond anyone's understanding. All that was known with any certainty was that they were always back within a day, or two at the outside.

Masklin looked down at the truck that now contained the explorer. Where would it go, what would happen to it? What would Angalo *see* before he came back again? If he didn't come back, what would Masklin tell his parents? That someone had to go, that he'd *begged* to go, that they had to see how a truck was driven, that everything depended on Angalo now? Still, he knew, it wouldn't sound very convincing in those circumstances.

Dorcas leaned over next to him.

"It'll be a job and a half getting everyone down this way." he said.

"I know. We'll have to think of some better way."

The inventor pointed down toward one of the other silent trucks. "There's a little step there," he said, "just by the driver's door, look. If we could get to that and get a rope around the handle . . ."

Masklin shook his head.

"It's too far up," he said. "It's a small step for a man, but a giant leap for nomekind."

Nine

V. Thus the Outsider said, Those who
believe *not* in the Outside, see, one will
be sent Outside to prove this thing;
VI. And one went upon a truck, and went
Outside, to see where there might be a
new Home;
VII. And there was much waiting, for he did
not return.

—*From The Book of Nome, Marketing v.
V–VII*

Masklin had taken to sleeping in an old
shoe box in the Stationeri Department, where he
could find a little peace. But when he got back
there was a small deputation of nomes waiting for
him. They were holding a book between them.

Masklin was getting a bit disillusioned with the
books. Maybe all the things he wanted to know
were written down somewhere, but the real prob-

lem was to find them. The books might have been put together especially to make it difficult to find things out. There seemed to be no sense in them. Or, rather, there was sense, but in nonsensical ways.

He recognized Vinto Pimmie, a very young Ironmongri. He sighed. Vinto was one of the keenest and fastest readers, just not a particularly good one, and he tended to get carried away.

"I've cracked it," said the boy proudly.

"Can you repair it?" said Masklin.

"I *mean*, I know how we can get a human to drive the truck for us!"

Masklin sighed. "We've thought about this, but it really won't work. If we show ourselves to a human—"

"Don't matter! Don't matter! He won't do anything, the reason being, we'll have—you'll like this —we'll have a gnu!"

Vinto beamed at him like a dog who's just done a difficult trick.

"A gnu," repeated Masklin weakly.

"Yes! It's in this book!" Vinto proudly displayed it. Masklin craned to see. He was picking reading up as he went along, a little bit at a time, but as far as he could make out the book was about *Host Age at 10,000 Feet.*

"It's got something to do with lots of shoes?" he said hopefully.

"No, no, no, what you do is, you get a gnu,

then you point it at the driver and someone says 'Look out, he's got a gnu!' and you say 'Take us where we want to go or I'll fire this gnu at you!' and then he—"

"Right, right. Fine," said Masklin, backing away. "Jolly good. Splendid idea. We'll definitely give it some thought. Well done."

"That was clever of me, wasn't it?" said Vinto, jumping from one foot to the other.

"Yes. Certainly. Er. You don't think you might be better reading a more *practical* kind of . . ." Masklin hesitated. Who knew what kind of books were best?

He staggered inside his box and pulled the cardboard over the door and leaned against it.

"Thing?" he said.

"*I hear you, Masklin,*" said the Thing from the heap of rags that was Masklin's bed.

"What's a gnu?"

There was a brief pause. Then the Thing said, "*The gnu, a member of the genus* Connochaetes *and the family* gnou, *is an African antelope often found in herds. Body length is up to 2 meters (6.5 feet), the shoulder height is about 140 centimeters (4.5 feet), and weight is up to 270 kilograms (600 pounds). Gnus inhabit the plains of central and southern Africa.*"

"Oh. Could you threaten someone with one?"

"*Quite possibly.*"

"Would there be one in the Store?"

There was another pause. *"Is there a Pet Department?"*

Masklin knew what that was. The subject had come up yesterday when Vinto had suggested taking a herd of guinea pigs to raise for meat.

"No," he said.

"Then I should think the chance is remote."

"Oh. Just as well, really." Masklin sagged down on his bed. "You see," he said, "we've got to be able to control where we're going. We need to find somewhere a little way from humans. But not too far. Somewhere safe."

"You must look for an atlas or map."

"What do they look like?"

"They may have the words Atlas *or* map *written on them."*

"I'll ask the Abbot to have a search made." Masklin yawned.

"You must sleep," said the Thing.

"People always want me to do things. Anyway, you don't sleep."

"It's different for me."

"What I need," said Masklin, "is a way. We can't use a gnu. They all think I know the way to do it and I don't know the way. We know what we need, but we'll never get it all into a truck in one night. They all think I know all the answers, but I don't. And I don't know the way. . . ."

He fell asleep and dreamed of being human-sized. Everything was so easy if you were human-sized.

Two days went past. The nomes kept watch from the girder over the garage. A small plastic telescope was rolled down from the Toy Department, and with its help the news came back that the big metal doors to the garage opened themselves when a human pressed a red button next to them. How could you press a button ten times higher than your head? It went down on Masklin's list of problems to solve.

Gurder found a map. It was in quite a small book.

"That was *no* trouble," he said. "We have dozens of these every year. It's called"—he read the gold lettering slowly—"*Pocket Diary*. And it has all this map at the back, look."

Masklin stared down at the small pages of blue and red blobs. Some of the blobs had names, like Africa and Asia.

"We-ell," he said, ". . . Ye-ss. I suppose so. Well done. Where are we, exactly?"

"In the middle," said Gurder promptly. "That's logical."

And then the truck returned.

Angalo didn't.

Masklin ran along the girder without thinking of the drop on either side. The little knot of figures told him everything he didn't want to know. A young nome who had just been lowered over the edge was sitting down and getting his breath back.

"I tried all the windows," he said. "They're all shut. Couldn't see anyone in there. It's very dark."

"Are you sure it's the right truck?" said Masklin to the head watcher.

"They've all got numbers on the front of them," he was told. "I was particularly sure to remember the one he went out on so when it come back this afternoon I—"

"We've got to get inside to have a look," said Masklin firmly. "Someone go and get . . . no, it'll take too long. Lower me down."

"What?"

"Lower me down," Masklin repeated. "All the way to the floor."

"It's a long way down," said one of them doubtfully.

"I know! Far too long to go all the way around by the stairs." Masklin handed the end of the thread to a couple of nomes. "He could be in there hurt, or anything."

" 'Tisn't our fault," said a nome. "There were humans all over the place when it came in. We had to wait."

"It's no one's fault. Some of you, go around the long way and meet me down there. Don't look so upset, it's no one's fault."

Except perhaps mine, he thought, as he spun around in the darkness. He watched the huge shadowy bulk of the truck slide past him. Somehow, they'd looked smaller outside.

The floor was greasy with *all*. He ran under the truck into a world roofed with wires and pipes, far too high to reach, but he poked around near one of the benches and came back dragging a length of wire and, with great difficulty, bent it into a hook at one end.

A moment later he was crawling among the pipes. It wasn't hard. Most of the underneath of the truck seemed to be pipes or wires, and after a minute or two he found a metal wall ahead of him with holes in it to take even more bundles of wires. It was possible, with a certain amount of pain, to squeeze through. Inside . . .

There was carpet. Odd thing to find in a truck. Here and there a candy wrapper lay, large as a newspaper to a nome. Huge pedal-shaped things stuck out of greasy holes in the floor. In the distance was a seat behind a huge wheel. Presumably it was something for the human in the truck to hold on to, Masklin thought.

"Angalo?" he called out softly.

There was no answer. He poked around aimlessly for a while, and had nearly given up when he spotted something in the drifts of fluff and paper under the seat. A human would have thought it was just another scrap of trash. Masklin recognized Angalo's coat.

He looked carefully at the trash. It was just possible to imagine someone had been lying there, watching. He rummaged among the trash and found a sandwich wrapper.

He took the coat back out with him; there didn't seem to be much else to do.

A dozen nomes were waiting anxiously on the *all*-soaked floor under the engine. Masklin held out the coat and shrugged.

"No sign," he said. "He's been there, but he's not there now."

"What could have happened to him?" said one of the older nomes.

Someone behind him said darkly, "Perhaps the Rain squashed him. Or he was blown away by the fierce Wind."

"That's right," said one of the others. "There could be dreadful things Outside."

"No!" said Masklin. "I mean, there *are* dreadful things—"

"Ah," said the nomes, nodding.

"—but not like that! He should have been perfectly all right if he stayed in the truck! I told him not to go exploring . . ."

He was aware of a sudden silence. The nomes weren't looking at him but past him, at something behind him.

The Duke de Haberdasheri was standing there

with some of his soldiers. He stared woodenly at Masklin, and then held out his hands without saying a word.

Masklin gave him the coat. The Duke turned it over and over, staring at it. The silence stretched out thinner and thinner, until it almost hummed.

"I forbade him to go," said the Duke softly. "I told him it would be dangerous. You know, that was foolish of me. It just made him more determined." He looked back up at Masklin.

"Well?" he said.

"Er?" said Masklin.

"Is my son still alive?"

"Um. He could be. There's no reason why not."

The Duke nodded vaguely.

This is it, thought Masklin. It's all going to end here.

The Duke stared up at the truck, and then looked around at his guards.

"And these things go Outside, do they?" he said.

"Oh, yes. All the time," said Masklin.

The Duke made an odd noise in the back of his throat.

"There is nothing Outside," he said. "I know this. But my son knew differently. You think we should go Outside. Will I see my son then?"

Masklin looked into the old man's eyes. They were like two eggs that weren't quite cooked yet.

And he thought about the size of everything Outside and the size of a nome. And then he thought, A leader should know all about truth and honesty and when to see the difference. Honestly, the chance of finding Angalo out there is greater than the whole Store taking wings and flying, but the *truth* is that . . .

"It's possible," he said, and felt terrible. But it *was* possible.

"Very well," said the Duke, his expression unchanged. "What do you need?"

"What?" said Masklin, his mouth dropping open.

"I said, what do you need? To make the truck go Outside?" said the Duke.

Masklin floundered. "Well, er, at the moment, I suppose, we need people—"

"How many?" snapped the Duke.

Masklin's mind raced.

"Fifty?" he ventured.

"You shall have them."

"But . . ." Masklin began. The Duke's expression changed now. He no longer looked totally lost and alone. Now he looked his usual angry self.

"Succeed," he hissed, and spun on his heel and stalked off.

That evening fifty Haberdasheri turned up, gawking at the garage and acting generally bewildered. Gurder protested, but Masklin put all those who looked even vaguely capable on to the reading scheme.

"There's too many!" said Gurder. "And they're common soldiers, for Arnold Bros. (est. 1905)'s sake!"

"I expected him to say fifty was too many and beat me down to twenty or so," said Masklin. "But I think we will need them all soon."

The reading program wasn't going the way he expected. There *were* useful things in books, it was true, but it was a hard job to find them among all the strange stuff.

Like the girl in the rabbit hole.

It was Vinto was came up with *that* one.

". . . and she fell down this hole and there was a white rabbit with a watch, I know about rabbits, and then she found this little bottle of stuff that made her BIG, I mean really huge, and then she found some more stuff that made her really small," he'd said breathlessly, his face glowing with enthusiasm. "So, all we need do *is*, we just find some of the BIG stuff and then one of us can drive the truck."

Masklin didn't dare ignore it. If just one nome could be made the size of a human, it would be *easy*. He'd told himself that dozens of times. It had to be worth an effort.

So they'd spent nearly all that night searching the Store for any bottles labeled "Drink Me." Either the Store didn't have it—and Gurder wasn't prepared to accept that, because the Store had Everything Under One Roof—or it just wasn't real. There seemed to be lots of things in books that weren't real. It was hard to see why Arnold Bros. (est. 1905) had put so many unreal things in books.

"So the faithful can tell the difference," Gurder had said.

Masklin had taken one book himself. It just fit his box. It was called *A Child's Guide to the Stars* and most of it was pictures of the sky at night. He knew that was real.

He liked to look at it when he had too much to think about. He looked at it now.

They had names, like Sirius and Rigel or Wolf 359 or Ross 154.

He tried a few on the Thing.

"*I do not know the names,*" it said.

"I thought we came from one of them," said Masklin, "You said—"

"*They are different names. Currently I cannot identify them.*"

"What was the name of the star that nomes came from?" said Masklin, lying back in the darkness.

"*It was called the Sun.*"

"But the sun's here!"

"*All stars are called the Sun by the people who live nearby. It is because they believe them to be important.*"

"Did they—I mean, did we visit many?"

"I have 94,563 registered as having been visited by nomes."

Masklin stared up at the darkness. Big numbers gave him trouble, but he could see that this number was one of the biggest. Bargains Galore! he thought, and then felt embarrassed and corrected it to Gosh! All those suns, miles apart, and all I have to do is move one truck!

Put like that, it seemed ridiculous.

Ten

X. When Lo! One returned, saying, I have gone upon Wheels, and I have seen the Outside.

XI. And they said to him, What is the Outside?

XII. And he said, It is Big.

—*From The Book of Nome, Accounts v. X–XII*

On the fourth day Angalo returned, wild-eyed and grinning like a maniac.

The nome on guard came running into the department, with Angalo swaggering behind him and a gaggle of younger nomes trailing, fascinated, in his wake. He was grimy and ragged and looked as though he hadn't slept for hours—but he walked proudly, with a strange swaying motion, like a nome who has boldly gone where no nome has gone before and can't wait to be asked about it.

"Where've I been?" he said. "Where've I *been*?

Where haven't I been, more like. You should see what's out there!"

"What?" they asked.

"Everywhere!" he said, his eyes glowing. "And you know what?"

"What?" they chorused.

"I've seen the Store from the *Outside*! It's"—he lowered his voice—"it's beautiful. All columns and big glass windows full of color!"

Now he was the center of a growing crowd as the news spread.

"Did you see all the departments?" said a Stationeri.

"No!"

"What?"

"You can't see the departments from Outside! It's just one big thing! And, and"—in the sudden silence he fumbled in his pouch for his notebook, which was now a lot fatter, and thumbed through the pages—"it's got a great big sign outside it and I copied it down because it's not trucker language and I didn't understand it but this is what it was."

He held it up.

The silence got deeper. Quite a few nomes could read by now.

The words said CLOSING-DOWN SALE.

Then he went to bed, still babbling excitedly about trucks and hills and cities, whatever they were, and slept for two hours.

Later on Masklin went to see him.

Angalo was sitting up in bed, his eyes still shining like bright marbles in the paleness of his face.

"Don't you get him tired," warned Granny Morkie, who always nursed anyone too ill to prevent it. "He's very weak and feverish, it's all the rattling around in those great noisy things, it's not natural. I've just had his dad in here, and I had to kick him out after five minutes."

"You got rid of the Duke?" said Masklin. "But how? He doesn't listen to anyone!"

"He might be a big nome in the Store," said Granny in a self-satisfied tone of voice, "but he's just an awkward nuisance in a sickroom."

"I need to talk to him," said Masklin.

"And I want to talk!" said Angalo, sitting up. "I want to tell everyone! There's everything out there! Some of the things I've seen . . . !"

"You just settle down," said Granny, gently pushing him back into the pillows. "And I'm not too happy about rats in here, either." Bobo's whiskers could just be seen under the end of the blankets.

"But he's very clean and he's my friend," said Angalo. "And you said you like rats."

"*Rat.* I said *rat.* Not rats," said Granny. She prodded Masklin. "Don't you let him get overexcited," she commanded.

Masklin sat down by the bed while Angalo talked with wild enthusiasm about the world outside, like someone who had spent his life with a blindfold on and had just been allowed to see. He talked about the big light in the sky, and roads full of trucks, and big things sticking out of the floor that had green things all over them—

"Trees," said Masklin.

—and great buildings where things went on the truck or came off it. It was at one of these that Angalo got lost. He'd climbed out to go to the lavatory when it stopped for a while and hadn't been able to get back before the driver returned and drove away. So he'd climbed onto another one, and some time after it had driven away it stopped at a big parking lot with other trucks in it. He started looking for another Arnold Bros. (est. 1905) truck.

"It must have been a diner on a highway," said Masklin. "We used to live near one."

"Is that what it's called?" said Angalo, hardly listening. "There was this big blue sign with pictures of cups and knives and forks on it. Anyway—"

—there weren't any Store trucks. Or perhaps there were, but there were so many other types he couldn't find one. Eventually he'd camped out on the edge of the truck parking lot, living on scraps, until by sheer luck one had turned up. He hadn't been able to get into the cab, but he had managed to climb up a tire and find a dark place where he had to hold on to cables with his hands and knees to stop himself from falling off onto the rushing road far below.

Angalo produced his notebook. It was stained almost black.

"Nearly lost it," he said. "Nearly *ate* it once, I was so hungry."

"Yes, but the actual driving," Masklin said insistently, with one eye on the impatient Granny Morkie. "How do they do the actual driving?"

Angalo flicked through the book. "I made a note somewhere," he said. "Ah, here." He passed it over.

Masklin looked at a complicated sketch of levers and arrows and numbers.

" 'Turn the key . . . one, two . . . press the red button . . . one, two . . . push pedal number one down with left foot, push big lever left and up . . . one, two . . . let pedal one up gently, push pedal number two down. . . .' " He gave up. "What does it all mean?" he said, dreading the answer. He knew what it was going to be.

"It's how you drive a truck," said Angalo.

"Oh. But, er, all these pedals and buttons and levers and things," said Masklin weakly.

"You need 'em all," said Angalo proudly, "and then you go rushing along, and you change up the gears, and—"

"Yes. Oh. I see," said Masklin, staring at the piece of paper.

How? he thought.

Angalo had been very thorough. Once, when he'd been alone in the cab, he'd measured the height of what he called the Gear Lever, which seemed very important. It was four times the height of a nome. And the big wheel that moved and seemed to be very important was as wide as eight nomes standing side by side.

And you had to have keys. Masklin hadn't known about the keys. He hadn't known about *anything*.

"I did well, didn't I?" said Angalo. "It's all in there."

"Yes. Yes. You did very well."

"You have a good look, it's all in there. All about the going-around-corners flasher and the horn," Angalo went on enthusiastically.

"Yes. Yes, I'm sure it is."

"And the go-faster pedal and the go-slower pedal and everything! Only you don't look very pleased."

"You've given me a lot to think about, I'm sure."

Angalo grabbed him by the sleeve. "They said there was only one Store," he said urgently. "There isn't, there's so much Outside, so much. There's other stores. I saw some. There could be nomes living in 'em! Life in other stores! Of course *you* know."

"You get some more sleep," said Masklin as kindly as he could manage.

"When are we going to go?"

"There's plenty of time," said Masklin. "Don't worry about it. Get some sleep."

He wandered out of the sickroom and straight into an argument. The Duke had returned, with some followers, and wanted to take Angalo up to the Stationeri Department. He was arguing with Granny Morkie. Or trying to, anyway.

"Madam, I assure you he'll be well looked after!" he was saying.

"Humph! Wot do you people know about doctrin'? You hardly ever have anything go wrong here! Where *I* come from," said Granny proudly, "it's sick, sick, sick all year round. Colds and sprains and bellyache and bites the whole time. That's what you call *experience*. I reckon I've seen more ill people than you've had hot dinners and"—she prodded the Duke in the stomach—"you've had a few of those."

"Madam, I could have you imprisoned!" roared the Duke.

Granny sniffed. "And what has that got to do with it?" she said.

The Duke opened his mouth to roar back, and then caught sight of Masklin. He shut it again.

"Very well," he said. "You are, in fact, quite right. But I will visit him every day."

"No longer than two minutes, mind," Granny warned.

"Five!" said the Duke.

"Three," said Granny.

"Four," they agreed.

The Duke nodded and beckoned Masklin toward him.

"You have spoken to my son," he said.

"Yes, sir," said Masklin.

"And he told you what he saw."

"Yes, sir."

The Duke looked quite small. Masklin had always thought of him as a big nome, but now he realized that most of the size was a sort of inward inflation, as if the nome was pumped up with importance and authority. It had gone now. The Duke looked worried and uncertain.

"Ah," he said, looking approximately at Masklin's left ear. "I think I sent you some people, didn't I?"

"Yes."

"Satisfactory, are they?"

"Yes, sir."

"Let me know if you need any more help, won't you? Any help at all." The Duke's voice faded to a mumble. He patted Masklin vaguely on the shoulder and wandered away.

"What's up with him?" said Masklin.

Granny Morkie started to roll bandages in a businesslike way. No one needed them, but she believed in having a good supply. Enough for the whole world, apparently.

"He's having to think," she said. "That always worries people."

"I just never thought it would be as hard as this!" Masklin wailed.

"You mean you didn't have any idea how we could drive a truck?" said Gurder.

"None at all?" said Grimma.

"I . . . well, I suppose I thought the trucks sort of went where you wanted," said Masklin. "I thought if they did it for humans, they'd do it for us. I didn't expect all this go-one-two-pull stuff! Those wheels and pedals are huge, I've seen them!"

He stared distractedly at their faces.

"I've thought about it for ages," he said. He felt they were the only two he could trust.

The cardboard door slid open and a small, cheerful face appeared.

"You'll like this one, Mr. Masklin," he said, "I've been doing some more reading."

"Not now, Vinto. We're a bit busy," said Masklin. Vinto's face fell.

"Oh, you might as well listen to him," said Grimma. "It's not as if we've got anything more important to do *now*."

Masklin hung his head.

"Well, lad," said Gurder with forced cheerfulness, "what idea have you come with this time, eh? Pulling the truck with wild hamsters, eh?"

"No, sir," said Vinto.

"Maybe you think we could make it grow wings and fly away in the sky?"

"No, sir. I found this book, it's how to capture humans, sir. And then we can get a gnu . . ."

Masklin gave the others a sick little smile.

"I explained to him that we can't use humans," he said. "I told you, Vinto. And I'm really not certain about threatening people with antelopes. . . ."

With a grunt of effort, the boy swung the book open.

"It's got this picture in it, sir."

They looked at the picture. It showed a human lying down. He was surrounded by nomes and covered with ropes.

"Gosh," said Grimma, "they've got books with pictures of us!"

"Oh, I know this one," said Gurder dismissively. "It's *Gulliver's Travels*. It's just stories, it's not real."

"Pictures of us in a book," said Grimma. "Imagine that. You see it, Masklin?"

Masklin stared.

"Yes, you're a good boy, well done," said Gurder, his voice sounding far off. "Thank you very much, Vinto, and now please go away."

Masklin stared. His mouth dropped open. He felt the ideas fizz up inside him and slosh into his head.

"The ropes," he said.

"It's just a picture," said Gurder.

"The ropes! Grimma, the ropes!"

"The ropes?"

Masklin raised his fists and stared up at the ceiling. At times like this it was almost possible to believe that there *was* someone up there above Kiddies Klothes.

"I can see the way!" he shouted while the three of them watched in astonishment. "I can see the way! Arnold Bros. (est. 1905), *I can see the way!*"

After Closing Time that evening several dozen small and stealthy figures crept across the garage floor and disappeared under one of the parked trucks. Anyone listening would have heard the occasional tiny clink, thud, or swear word. After ten minutes they were in the cab.

They stood in wonder, looking around.

Masklin wandered over to one of the pedals, which was taller than he was, and gave it an experimental push. It didn't so much as wobble. Several of the others came over and helped and managed to get it to move a little.

One nome stood and watched them thoughtfully. It was Dorcas, wearing his belt from which hung a variety of homemade tools, and he was idly twiddling a pencil lead he kept permanently behind one ear when it wasn't being used.

Masklin walked back to him.

"What d'you think?" he said.

Dorcas rubbed his nose. "It's all down to levers and pulleys," he said. "Amazing things, levers.

Give me a lever long enough, and a firm enough place to stand, and I could move the Store."

"Just one of these pedals would be enough for now," said Masklin politely.

Dorcas nodded. "We'll give it a try," he said. "All right, lads. Bring it up."

A piece of wood, carried all the way down from the Home Handyman Department, was nomehandled into the cab. Dorcas ambled around, measuring distances with a piece of thread, and finally had them wedge one end of the wood into a crack in the metal floor. Four nomes stationed themselves at the other end and hauled the wood across until it was resting on the lever.

"Right, lads," said Dorcas again.

They pushed down. The pedal went all the way to the floor. There was a ragged cheer.

"How did you *do* that?" said Masklin.

"That's levers for you," said Dorcas. "*O*-kay." He looked around, scratching his chin. "So we'll need three levers." He looked up at the great circle of the steering wheel. "You have any ideas about that?" he said.

"I thought ropes," said Masklin.

"How d'you mean?"

"It's got those spokes in it, so if we tie ropes to them and have teams of nomes on the ropes, they could pull it one way or the other and that'll make the truck go the way we want," said Masklin.

Dorcas squinted at the wheel. He paced the

floor. He looked up. He looked down. His lips moved as he worked things out.

"They won't see where they're going," he said finally.

"I thought someone could stand right up there, by the big window in the front, and sort of tell them what to do," said Masklin, looking hopefully at the old nome.

"These're powerful noisy things, Angalo says," said Dorcas. He scratched his chin again. "I reckon I can do something about that. There's this big lever here, the Beer Lever—"

"Gear Lever," said Masklin.

"Ah. Roped again?"

"I thought so," said Masklin earnestly. "What do *you* think?"

Dorcas sucked in his breath. "We-ell," he said, "what with teams pulling the wheels, and teams shifting the Gear Lever, and people working the pedals with levers, and someone up there telling them all what to do, it's going to take a powerful lot of practicing. Supposing I rig up all the tackle, all the ropes and such . . . how many nights will we have to practice? You know, get the hang of it?"

"Including the night we, er, leave?"

"Yes," said Dorcas.

"One," said Masklin.

Dorcas sniffed. He stared upward for a while, humming under his breath.

"It's impossible," he said.

"We'll only have one chance, you see," said Masklin. "If it's a problem with all the equipment—"

"Oh, no problem there," said Dorcas. "That's just pieces of wood and string, I can have that ready by tomorrow. I was thinking of the people, see. You're going to need a powerful lot of nomes to do all this. And *they're* going to need training."

"But, but all that they'll have to do is pull and push when they're told, won't they?"

Dorcas hummed under his breath again. Masklin got the impression that he always did that if he was going to break some bad news.

"Well, laddie," he said. "I'm six, I've seen a lot of people, and I've got to tell you, if you lined up ten nomes and shouted 'Pull!' four of them would push and two of them would say 'Pardon?' That's how people are. It's just nomish nature."

He grinned at Masklin's crestfallen expression.

"What you ought to do," he said, "is find us a little truck to practice on."

Masklin nodded gloomily.

"And," said Dorcas, "have you thought again about how you're going to get everyone on? Two thousand nomes, mind. Plus all this stuff we're taking. You can't have old grannies and little babies shinnying up ropes or crawling through holes, can you?"

Masklin shook his head. Dorcas was watching him with his normal mild grin

This nome, Masklin thought, knows his stuff. But if I say to him Leave it all to me, he'll leave it all to me, just to serve me right. Oh, Critical Path Analysis! Why is it always people?

"Have you got any ideas?" he said. "I really would appreciate your help."

Dorcas gave him a long thoughtful look, and then patted him on the shoulder.

"I've been looking around this place," he said. "Maybe there's a way we can practice *and* solve the other problem. You come down here again tomorrow night and we'll see, shall we?"

Masklin nodded.

The trouble was, he thought as he walked back, that there weren't enough people. A lot of the Ironmongri were helping, and some of the other departments, and quite a few young nomes were sneaking off to help because it was all exciting and unusual. As far as the rest of them were concerned, though, life was going on as normal.

In fact, the Store was, if anything, busier than usual.

Of all the family heads, only the Count seemed at all willing to take an interest, and Masklin suspected that even he didn't really think the Store was going to end. It just meant that the Ironmongri could learn to read and it annoyed the

Haberdasheri, which amused the Count. Even Gurder didn't seem as sure as he had been.

Masklin went back to his box and slept and woke up an hour later.

The terror had started.

Eleven

Run to the Elevators,
Elevators, won't you carry me?
Run to the walls,
Walls, won't you hide me?
Run to the truck,
Truck, won't you take me?
All on that Day.

—From The Book of Nome, Exits Chap. 1, v. I

It started with silence when there should have been noise. All the nomes were used to the distant thumping and murmuring of the humans during the long daylight hours, so they didn't notice it. Now that it was gone they could hear the strange, oppressive silence. There were days, of course, when humans didn't come into the Store— for instance, Arnold Bros. (est. 1905) sometimes allowed them almost a week off between the excitement of Christmas Fayre and the hurly-burly of

Winter Sale Starts Today! But the nomes were used to this, it was part of the gentle rhythm of Store life. This wasn't the right day.

After several hours of silence they stopped telling one another not to worry, it was probably just some special day or something, like that time when the Store had shut for a week for redecoration, and one or two of the braver or more inquisitive ones risked a quick glance above floor level.

Emptiness stretched away between the familiar counters. And there didn't seem to be much stock around.

"It's always like this after a sale," they said. "And then, before you know where you are, all the shelves are filled up again. Nothing to get upset about at all. It's all part of Arnold Bros. (est. 1905)'s great plan."

And they sat in silence, or hummed a little tune, or found something to occupy their minds to stop them from thinking unpleasant thoughts. It didn't work.

And then, when the humans came in and started taking the few things that *were* left off the shelves and counters and piling them in great boxes and taking them down to the garage and loading them into the trucks . . .

And started taking up the floorboards . . .

Masklin awoke. People were prodding him. Somewhere in the distance other people were shouting. It was somehow familiar.

"Get up, quickly!" said Gurder.

"What's happening?" said Masklin, yawning.

"Humans are taking the Store to bits!"

Masklin sat bolt upright.

"They can't be! It's not time!" he said.

"They're doing it just the same!"

Masklin stood up, struggling into his clothes. He jigged sideways across the floor, one leg out of his trousers, and thumped the Thing.

"Hey!" he said. "You said demolition wasn't for ages yet!"

"Fourteen days," said the Thing.

"It's starting *now!*"

"This is probably the preparatory work and removal of remaining stock to new premises," said the Thing.

"Oh, good. That should make everyone feel a lot better. Why didn't you tell us?"

"I was not aware you did not know."

"Well, we didn't. So what do you suggest we do now?"

"Leave as soon as possible."

Masklin snarled. He had expected two more weeks to solve all the problems. They could have stockpiled stuff to take with them. They could have made the right plans. Even two weeks was hardly long enough. Now even the thought of one week was a luxury.

He went out into the milling, disorganized crowd. Fortunately the boards hadn't been taken up in an inhabited area—some of the more sensible refugees said that only a few had been taken up in the far end of the Gardening Department so the humans could get at the water pipes—but nomes living nearby were taking no chances.

There was a thump overhead. A few minutes later a breathless nome arrived and reported that the carpets were being rolled up and taken away.

That caused a terrified silence. Masklin realized that they were all looking at him.

"Er," he said.

Then he said, "I think everyone ought to get as much food as he can carry and go down to the Basement, near the garage."

"You mean you still think we should do *it*?" said Gurder.

"We haven't much choice, have we?"

"But we were—you said we should take as much as we could from the Store, all the wire and tools and things. And books," said Gurder.

"We'll be lucky if we can just take ourselves. There's no *time*!"

Another messenger came running up. It was one of Dorcas's group. He whispered something to Masklin, who gave a strange smile.

"Can it be that Arnold Bros. (est. 1905) has abandoned us in our hour of need?" said Gurder.

"I don't think so. He may be helping us," said Masklin. "Because, well, you'll never guess where the humans are putting all this stuff. . . ."

Twelve

I. And the Outsider said, Glory to the name of Arnold Bros. (est. 1905).
II. For he hath sent us a Truck, and the Humans are loading it now with all manner of Things needful to nomes. It is a Sign. Everything *Must* Go. Including us.

—*From The Book of Nome, Exits Chap. 2 v. I–II*

Half an hour later Masklin lay on the girder with Dorcas, looking down at the garage.

He had never seen it so busy. Humans sleep-walked across the floor, carrying bundles of carpet into the backs of some of the trucks. Yellow things, like a cross between a very small truck and a very large armchair, inched around them, stacking boxes.

Dorcas passed him the telescope.

"Busy little things, ain't they?" he said conversationally. "Been at it all morning, they have. A couple of trucks have already gone out and come back, so they can't be going very far."

"The letter we saw said something about a new store," said Masklin. "Perhaps they're taking the stuff there."

"Could be. It's mostly carpets at the moment, and some of the big frozen humans from Fashions."

Masklin made a face. According to Gurder, the big pink humans that stood in Fashions and Kiddies Klothes and Young Living, and never moved at all, were those who had incurred Arnold Bros. (est. 1905)'s displeasure. They had been turned into horrible pink stuff, and some said they could even be taken apart. But certain Klothian philosophers said no, they were particularly *good* humans who had been allowed to stay in the Store forever and not made to disappear at Closing Time. Religion was very hard to understand.

As Masklin watched the big roller door creaked upward and a truck nearby started with a roar and ground slowly out into the blinding daylight.

"What we need," he said, "is a truck with a lot of stuff from the Ironmongri Department. Wire, you know, and tools and things. Have you seen any food?"

"Looked like a lot of stuff from the Food Hall on the first truck out," said Dorcas.

"We'll have to make do, then."

"What'll I do," said Dorcas slowly, "if they load it all up on a truck and drive it away? They're working powerful fast, for humans."

"Surely they can't empty the Store in one day?" said Masklin.

Dorcas shrugged.

"Who knows?" he said.

"You'll have to stop the truck from leaving," said Masklin.

"How? By throwing myself under it?"

"Any way you can think of," said Masklin.

Dorcas grinned. "I'll find a way. The lads are getting used to this place."

Refugees were flowing into the Ironmongri Department from all over the Store, filling all the space under the floor with a frightened buzz of whispered conversation. Many of them looked up as Masklin walked past, and what he saw in their faces terrified him.

They believe I can help, he thought. They're looking at me as if I'm their only hope. And I don't know what to do. Probably none of it will work, we should have had more *time*.

He forced himself to look brimful of confidence, and it seemed to satisfy people. All they wanted to know was that someone, somewhere, knew what he was doing. Masklin wondered who it was; it certainly wasn't him.

The news was bad from everywhere. A lot of the Gardening Department had been cleared. Most of the clothes departments were empty. The counters were being ripped out of Cosmetics, although fortunately not many nomes lived there. Masklin could hear, even here, the thud and crunch of the work going on.

Finally he could stand it no longer. Too many people kept staring at him. He went back down to the garage, where Dorcas was still watching from his spy post on top of the girder.

"What's happened?" said Masklin. The old nomes pointed to the truck immediately below them.

"That's the one we want," he said. "It's got all sorts in it. Lots of stuff from the Do-It-Yourself Department. There's even some Haberdasheri things, needles and whatnot. All the stuff you told me to look out for."

"We've got to stop them from driving it out!" said Masklin.

Dorcas grinned.

"The machinery that raises the door won't work," he said. "The fuse has gone."

"What's a fuse?" said Masklin.

Dorcas picked up a long, thick red bar lying by his feet. "This is," he said.

"You took it?"

"Tricky job, we had to tie a bit of string around it. Made a powerful big spark when we pulled it out."

"But I expect they can put another one in," said Masklin.

"Oh, they did," said Dorcas with a self-satisfied expression, "they're not stupid. Didn't work, though, because after we took the fuse out the lads went and cut the wires inside the wall in a couple of places. Very dangerous, but it'll take the humans forever to find it."

"Hmm. But supposing they lever the door up?"

"Won't do them any good. It's not as if the truck will go, anyway."

"Why not?"

Dorcas pointed downward. Masklin watched, and after a moment saw a couple of small figures scurry out from under the truck and dive into the shadows by the wall.

They were carrying a pair of pliers.

A moment later a solitary figure hurried after them, dragging a length of wire.

"Powerful lot of wire them trucks need," said Dorcas. "This one ain't got so much, now. Funny, isn't it? Take away a tiny spark and the truck won't go. Don't worry, though, I reckon we'll know where to put it all back later."

"But you still need a key to start a truck," said Masklin sadly, "and I don't know where to get one."

"Ahem," said Dorcas. "I've been doing a bit of investigating there. You don't really need a key. A bit of wire will do, if you know where to put it. Don't fret about it."

There was a clang down below. One of the humans had given the door a kick.

"Temper, temper," said Dorcas mildly.

"You've thought of just about everything," said Masklin admiringly.

"I hope so," said Dorcas. "But we'd better make sure, hadn't we?" He stood up and produced a large white flag, which he waved over his head. There was an answering flicker of white from the shadows on the far side of the garage.

And then the lights went out.

"Useful thing, electricity," said Dorcas in the darkness. There was a rumble of annoyance from the humans below, and then a jangling noise as one of them walked into something. After some grunting and a few more thuds, one of the humans found a doorway out into the Basement, and the rest of them followed it.

"Don't you think they'll suspect something?" said Masklin.

"There's other humans working in the Store, they'll probably think they caused it," said Dorcas.

"That electricity is amazing stuff," said Masklin. "Can you make it? The Count de Ironmongri was very mysterious about it."

"That's because the Ironmongri don't know anything." Dorcas sniffed. "Just how to steal it. I've been looking at books. Making electricity is very simple, you know. You just need to get hold of some stuff called you-ranium. I think it's a kind of metal."

"Is there some in the Ironmongeri Department?" said Masklin hopefully.

"Apparently not," said Dorcas.

The Thing wasn't very helpful, either.

"I doubt if you are ready for nuclear power yet," it said. *"Try windmills."*

Masklin finished putting his possessions, such as they were, in a bag.

"When we leave," he said, "you won't be able to talk, will you? You need electricity to drink."

"That is the case, yes."

"Can't you tell us which way we should go?"

"No. However, I detect radio traffic indicative of airline activity to the north of here."

Masklin hesitated. "That's good, is it?"

"It means there are flying machines."

"And we can fly all the way home?" said Masklin.

"No. But they may be the next step. It may be possible to communicate with the starship. But first you must ride the truck."

"After that I should think anything is possible," said Masklin gloomily. He looked expectantly at the Thing, and then noticed with horror that its lights were going off one by one.

"Thing!"

"When you are successful we will talk again," said the Thing.

"But you're supposed to *help* us!" said Masklin.

"I suggest you consider deeply the proper meaning of the word help," said the box. *"Either you are intelligent nomes or just clever animals. It's up to you to find out which."*

"What?"

The last light went off.

"Thing?"

The lights stayed off. The little black box contrived to look extremely dead and silent.

"But I'd relied on you to help us sort out the driving and everything! You're just going to leave me like this?"

If anything, the box got darker. Masklin stared at it.

Then he thought, It's all very well for it. Everyone's relying on me. I've got no one to rely on. I wonder if the old Abbot felt like this. I wonder how he stood it for so long. It's always me who has to do everything, no one ever thinks about me or what I want. . . .

The shabby cardboard door swung aside and Grimma stepped in.

She looked from the darkened Thing to Masklin.

"They're asking for you out there," she said quietly. "Why is the Thing all dark?"

"It just said good-bye! It said it won't help anymore!" Masklin wailed. "It just said we have to prove we can do things for ourselves and it will speak to us when we're successful! What shall I do?"

I know what I could do, he thought. I could do with a cool cloth on my forehead. I could do with a bit of understanding. I could do with a bit of sympathy. Good old Grimma. You can rely on her.

"What you'll do," she said sharply, "is stop moping and get up and go out there and *get things organized!*"

"Wha—"

"Figure things out! Make new plans! Give people orders! *Get on with it!*"

"But—"

"*Do it now!*" she snapped.

Masklin stood up.

"You shouldn't talk to me like that," he said plaintively. "I'm the leader, you know."

She stood, arms akimbo, glaring at him.

"Of course you're the leader," she said. "Did I say you weren't the leader? Everyone knows you're the leader! Now get out there and lead!"

He lurched past. She tapped him on the shoulder.

"And learn to listen," she added.

"Eh? What do you mean?"

"The Thing's a sort of thinking machine, isn't it? That's what Dorcas said. Well, machines say exactly what they mean, don't they?"

"Yes, I suppose so, but . . ."

Grimma gave him a bright, triumphant smile.

"Well, it said 'when,' " she said. "*Think* about it. It could have said 'if.' "

Night came. Masklin thought the humans were never going to leave. One of them, with a flashlight and a box of tools, spent a long time examining fuse boxes and peering at the wiring in the Basement. Now at last even it was gone, grumbling and slamming the door behind it.

After a little while the lights came on in the garage.

There was a rustling in the walls, and then a dark tide flowed out from under benches. Some of the young nomes in the lead carried hooks on the end of thread lines, which they swung up to the truck's covers. They caught, one after another, and the nomes swarmed up them. Other nomes brought thicker string, which was tied to the ends of the thread and gradually dragged upward.

Masklin ran along, under the endless shadow of the truck, to the oily darkness under the engine where Dorcas's teams were already dragging their equipment into position. Dorcas himself was in the cab, rooting around among the thick wires. There was a sizzling noise, and then the light in the cab came on.

"There," said Dorcas, "now we can see what we're at. Come on, lads! Let's have a bit of effort!"

When he turned around and saw Masklin he made as if to hide his hands behind his back and then thought better of it. Both of them were thrust into what Masklin could now see were the fingers cut out of rubber gloves.

"Ah," said Dorcas, "didn't know you were there. Bit of a trade secret, see? Electricity can't abide rubber. It stops the stuff from biting you." He ducked as a team of nomes swung a long wooden beam across the cab and started to fasten it to the Gear Lever.

"How long's it going to take?" shouted Masklin as another team ran past dragging a ball of string. There was quite a din in the cab now, and threads and pieces of wood were moving in every direction in what he hoped was an organized way.

"Could be an hour, maybe," said Dorcas, and added, not unkindly, "We'd get on quicker without people in the way."

Masklin nodded and explored the rear of the cab. The truck was old, and he found another hold for a bundle of wires that, at a squeeze, would take a nome as well. He crawled out into the open air and then found another gap that let him into the rear of the truck.

The first nomes aboard had dragged up one end of a thin piece of wood, which was acting as a gangplank. The rest were scrambling up it now.

Masklin had put Granny Morkie in charge of

this. The old woman had a natural talent for making frightened people do things.

"Steep?" she was shouting at a fat nome who had got halfway up and was clinging there in fright. "Call this steep? It ain't steep, it's a stroll! Want me to come down there and help you?"

The mere threat budged him from his perch and he nearly ran the rest of the way, ducking gratefully into the shadows of the cargo.

"Everyone had better try to find somewhere soft to lie down," said Masklin. "It could be a rough journey. And you must send all the strongest nomes up toward the cab. We're going to need everyone we can get, believe me."

She nodded, and then shouted at a family that was blocking the gangway.

Masklin looked down at the endless stream of people climbing into the truck, many of them staggering under the weight of possessions.

Funny, but now he felt he'd done everything he could. Everything was ticking over like a, like a, like something that went tick. Either all the plans would work or they wouldn't. Either the nomes could act together or they couldn't.

He recalled the picture of Gulliver. It probably wasn't real, Gurder had said. Books often had things in them that weren't really real. But it would be nice to think that nomes could agree on something long enough to be like the little people in the book. . . .

"Well, it's all going well, then," he said vaguely.

"Well enough." Granny nodded.

"It would be a good idea if we found out exactly what was in all these boxes and things," Masklin ventured, "because we might have to get out quickly when we stop and—"

"I told Torrit to see to it," said Granny. "Don't you worry about it."

"Oh," said Masklin weakly, "good."

He hadn't left himself anything to do.

He went back to the cab out of sheer—well, not boredom, because his heart was pounding like a drum, but out of restlessness.

Dorcas's nomes had already built a wooden platform above the steering wheel and right in front of the big window. Dorcas himself was back down on the floor of the cab, drilling the driving teams.

"Right!" he shouted. "Give me . . . First Gear!"

"Pedal down . . . two, three . . ." chorused the team on the Clutch Pedal.

"Pedal up . . . two, three . . ." shouted the Accelerator team.

"Lever up . . . two, three . . ." echoed the nomes by the Gear Lever.

"Pedal up . . . two, three, four!" The leader of the Clutch team threw Dorcas a salute. "Gears all changed, sir!" he shouted.

"That was terrible. Really terrible," said Dorcas. "What's happened to the Accelerator team, eh? Get that pedal down!"

"Sorry, Dorcas."

Masklin tapped Dorcas on the shoulder.

"Keep doing it!" Dorcas commanded. "I want you dead smooth all the way up to fourth. Yes? What? Oh, it's you."

"Yes, it's me. Everyone's nearly on," said Masklin. "When will you be ready?"

"This bunch won't be ready *ever.*"

"Oh."

"So we might as well start whenever you like and pick it up as we go along. We can't even *try* steering until it's moving, of course."

"We're going to send a lot more people to help you," said Masklin.

"Oh, good," said Dorcas. "Just what I need, lots more people who don't know their right from their left."

"How are you going to know which way to steer?"

"Semaphore," said Dorcas firmly.

"Semaphore?"

"Signaling with flags. You just tell my lad up on the platform what you want done and I'll watch the signals. If we'd had one more week, I reckon I could have rigged up some sort of telephone."

"Flags," said Masklin. "Will that work?"

"It'd better, hadn't it? We can give it a try later on."

•

And now it was later on. The last nome scouts had climbed aboard. In the back of the truck most of the people made themselves as comfortable as possible and lay, wide awake, in the darkness.

Masklin was up on the platform with Angalo, Gurder, and the Thing. Gurder knew even less about trucks than Masklin, but it was felt best to have him there, just in case. After all, they were stealing Arnold Bros. (est. 1905)'s truck. Someone might have to do some explaining. But he'd drawn the line about having Bobo in the cab. The rat was back with everyone else.

Grimma was there too. Gurder asked her what she was doing there. She asked him what *he* was doing there. They both looked at Masklin.

"She can help me with the reading," he said, secretly relieved. He wasn't, despite lots of effort, all that good at it. There seemed to be a knack he couldn't get the hang of. Grimma, on the other hand, seemed to do it now without thinking. If her brain was exploding, it was doing it in unnoticeable ways.

She nodded smugly and propped the High Way Code open in front of him.

"There's things you've got to do," he said uncertainly. "Before you start, you've got to look in a mur—"

"Mirror," said Grimma.

"—mirror. That's what it says here. Mirror," said Masklin firmly.

He looked inquiringly at Angalo, who shrugged.

"I don't know anything about that," he said. "My driver used to look at it, but I don't know why."

"Do you have to look for anything special? I mean, perhaps you have to make a face in it or something," said Masklin.

"Whatever it is, we'd better do things properly," said Gurder firmly. He pointed. "There's a mirror up there, near the ceiling."

"Daft place to put it," said Masklin. He managed to hook it with a grapnel and, after some effort, pulled himself up to it.

"Can you see anything?" Gurder called out.

"Just me."

"Well, come on back down. You've done it, that's the main thing."

Masklin slid back to the decking, which wobbled under him.

Grimma peered at the Code.

"Then you've got to signal your intentions," she said. "That's clear, anyway. Signaler?"

One of Dorcas's assistants stepped forward a bit uncertainly, holding his two white flags carefully downward.

"Yes, sir, ma'am?" he said.

"Tell Dorcas"—Grimma looked at the others— "tell him we're ready to start."

"Excuse *me*," said Gurder. "If it's anyone's job to tell them we're ready to start, it's *my* job to tell them we're ready to start. I want it to be quite clear that I'm the person who tells people to start." He looked sheepishly at Grimma. "Er. We're ready to start," he said.

"Right you are, ma'am." The signaler waved his arms briefly. From far below the engineer's voice boomed back, "Ready!"

"Well, then," said Masklin. "This is it, then."

"Yes," said Gurder, glaring at Grimma. "Is there anything we've forgotten?"

"Lots of things, probably," said Masklin.

"Too late now, at any rate," said Gurder.

"Yes."

"Yes."

"Right then."

"Right."

They stood in silence for a moment.

"Shall you give the order or shall I?" said Masklin.

"I was wondering whether to ask Arnold Bros. (est. 1905) to watch over us and keep us safe," said Gurder. "After all, we may be leaving the Store but this is still his truck." He grinned wretchedly and sighed. "I wish he'd give us some sort of sign," he said, "to show he approves."

"Ready when you are, up there!" shouted Dorcas.

Masklin went to the edge of the platform and leaned on the flimsy rail.

The whole of the floor of the cab was covered in nomes, holding ropes in readiness or waiting by their levers and pulleys. They stood in absolute silence in the shadows, but every face was turned upward so that Masklin looked down at a sea of frightened and excited blobs.

He waved his hand.

"Start the engine," he said, and his voice sounded unnaturally loud in the expectant silence.

He walked back and looked out into the bright emptiness of the garage. There were a few other trucks parked against the opposite wall, and one or two of the small yellow loading trucks stood where the humans had left them. To think he'd once called it a truck nest! *Garage*, that was the word. It was amazing, the feeling you got from knowing the right names. You felt in control. It was as if knowing what the right name was gave you a sort of lever.

There was a whirring noise from somewhere in front of them, and then the platform shook to a thunder roll. Unlike thunder, it didn't die away. The engine had started.

Masklin grabbed hold of the rail before he was shaken off and felt Angalo tug on his sleeve.

"It always sounds like this!" he shouted above the din. "You get used to it after a while!"

"Good!" It wasn't a noise. It was too loud to be called a noise. It was more like solid air.

"I think we'd better practice a bit! To get the hang of it! Shall I tell the signaler that we want to move forward very slowly?"

Masklin nodded grimly. The signaler thought for a moment, and then waved his flags.

Masklin could distantly hear Dorcas yelling orders. There was a grinding noise, followed by a jolt that almost knocked him over. He managed to land on his hands and knees and looked into Gurder's frightened face.

"We're moving!" shouted the Stationeri.

Masklin stared out the windshield.

"Yes, and you know what?" he yelled, springing up, "We're moving *backward*!"

Angalo staggered over to the signaler, who had dropped one of his flags.

"Forward slowly, I said! Forward slowly! Not backward! Forward!"

"I signaled forward!"

"But we're *going* backward! Signal them to go forward!"

The signaler scrabbled for his other flag and waved frantically at the teams below.

"No, don't signal forward, just signal them to sto—" Masklin began.

There was a sound from the far end of the

truck. The only word to describe it was *crunch*, but it's far too short and simple a word to describe the nasty, complicated, metallic noise and the jolt that threw Masklin on his stomach again. The engine stopped.

The echoes died away.

"Sorree!" Dorcas called out in the distance. They heard him talking in a low, menacing voice to the teams: "Satisfied? Satisfied, are we? When I said move the Gear Lever up and left and up I meant up and left and up, not up and right and up! Right?"

"Your right or our right, Dorcas?"

"Any right!"

"No, but—"

"Don't you but me!"

"Yes, but—"

Masklin and the others sat down as the argument skidded back and forth below them. Gurder was still lying on the planks.

"We actually moved!" he was whispering. "Arnold Bros. (est. 1905) *was* right. Everything *Must Go!*"

"I'd like it to go a little farther if it's all right by him," said Angalo grimly.

"Hello up there!" Dorcas's voice boomed with mad cheerfulness. "Little bit of teething trouble down here. All fixed now. Ready when you are!"

"Should I look in the mirror again, what do

you think?" said Masklin to Grimma. She shrugged.

"I shouldn't bother," said Angalo. "Let's just go forward. And as soon as possible, I think. I can smell diesel *all*.

We must have knocked over some drums of it or something."

"That's bad, is it?" said Masklin.

"It burns," said Angalo. "It just needs a spark or something to set it off."

The engine roared into life again. This time they did inch forward, after some grinding noises, and rolled across the floor until the truck was in front of the big steel door. It stopped with a slight jerk.

"Like to try a few practice turns," shouted Dorcas. "Smooth out a few rough edges!"

"I really think it would be a very bad idea to stay here," said Angalo urgently.

"You're right," said Masklin. "The sooner we get out of here the better. Signal Dorcas to open the door."

The signaler hesitated. "I don't think we've got a signal for that," he said. Masklin leaned over the rail.

"Dorcas!"

"Yes?"

"Open the door! We've got to get out *now*!"

The distant figure cupped its hand to its ear. "What?"

"I said open the door! It's urgent!"

Dorcas appeared to consider this for a while, and then raised his megaphone.

"You'll laugh when I tell you this," he said.

"What was that?" said Grimma.

"He said we're going to laugh," said Angalo.

"Oh. Good."

"Come *on!*" shouted Masklin. Dorcas's reply was lost in the din from the engine.

"What?" shouted Masklin.

"What?"

"What did you *say?*"

"I said, in all this rush I clean forgot about the door!"

"What'd he say?" said Gurder.

Masklin turned and looked at the door. Dorcas had been very proud of the way he'd kept it from opening. Now it had an extremely closed look. If something with no face could look smug, the door had managed it.

He turned back in exasperation, and also in time to see the small door to the rest of the Store swing slowly open. There was a figure there, behind a little circle of sharp white light.

His terrible light, Masklin thought again.

It was Prices Slashed.

Masklin felt his mind begin to think very clearly and slowly.

It's just a human, it said. It's nothing scary. Just a human, with its name on it in case it forgets who it is, like all those female humans in the Store with names like "Tracy" and "Sharon" and "Mrs. J. E. Williams, Supervisor." This is just old "Security" again. He lives down in the Boiler Room and drinks tea. He's heard the noise.

He's come to find out what made it.

That is, us.

"Oh, no," whispered Angalo as the figure lurched across the floor. "Do you see what it's got in its mouth?"

"It's a cigarette. I've seen humans with it before. What about it?" said Masklin.

"It's alight," said Angalo. "Do you think it can't even *smell* the diesel?"

"What happens if it catches alight, then?" said Masklin, suspecting that he knew the answer.

"It goes whoomph," said Angalo.

"Just whoomph?"

"Whoomph is enough."

The human came nearer. Masklin could see its eyes now. Humans weren't very good at seeing nomes even when they were standing still, but even a human would wonder why a truck was driving itself around its garage in the middle of the night.

Security reached the cab and reached out slowly for the door handle. His light shone in through the side window, and at that moment Gurder reared up, trembling with rage.

"Begone, foul fiend!" he yelled, illuminated as

if by a spotlight. "Heed ye the signs of Arnold Bros. (est. 1905)! *No Smoking! Exit This Way!*"

The human's face wrinkled in ponderous astonishment, and then, as slowly as the drift of clouds, it became an expression of panic. He let go of the door handle, turned, and began to head for the little door at what, for a human, was high speed. As he did so the glowing cigarette fell from his mouth and, turning over and over, dropped slowly toward the floor.

Masklin and Angalo looked at each, and then at the signaler.

"Go fast!" they shouted.

A moment later the entire truck juddered as the teams tackled the complicated process of changing gears. Then it rolled forward.

"Fast! I said fast!" Masklin shouted.

"What's going on?" shouted Dorcas. "What about the door?"

"We'll open the door! We'll open the door!" shouted Masklin.

"How?"

"Well, it didn't look very thick, did it?"

The world of nomes is, to humans, a rapid world. They live so fast that the things that happen around them seem quite slow, so the truck seemed to drift across the floor, up the ramp, and hit the door in a leisurely way. There was a long-drawn-out boom and the noise of bits of metal being torn apart, a scraping noise across the roof of the cab, and then there was no door at all, only darkness studded with light.

"Left! Go left!" Angalo screamed.

The truck skidded around slowly, bounced lazily off a wall, and rolled a little way down the street.

"Keep going! Keep going! Now straighten up!"

A bright light shone briefly on the wall outside the cab.

And then, behind them, a sound like *whoomph!*

Thirteen

I. Arnold Bros. (est. 1905) said, All is now
finished;

II. All curtains, carpeting, bedding, lingerie,
toys, millinery, haberdashery,
ironmongery, electrical;

III. All walls, floors, ceilings, elevators,
moving stairs;

IV. Everything Must Go.

*—From The Book of Nome, Exits Chap. 3, v.
I–IV*

Later on, when the next chapters of The
Book of Nome came to be written, they said the
end of the Store started with a bang. This wasn't
true, but was put in because *bang* sounded more
impressive. In fact, the ball of yellow and orange
fire that rolled out of the garage, carrying the remains of the door with it, just made a noise like a
giant dog gently clearing its throat.

Whoomph.

The nomes weren't in a position to take much notice of it at the time. They were more concerned with the noise made by other things nearly hitting them.

Masklin had been prepared for other vehicles on the road. The High Way Code had a lot to say about it. It was important not to drive into them. What was worrying him was the way they seemed determined to run into the truck. They emitted long blaring noises, like sick cows.

"Left a bit!" Angalo shouted. "Then right just a smidgen, then go straight!"

"Smidgen?" said the signaler slowly. "I don't think I know a code for smidgen. Could we—"

"Slow! Now left a bit! We've got to get on the right side of the street!"

Grimma peered over the top of the High Way Code.

"We *are* on the right side," she said.

"Yes, but the right side should be on the left side!"

Masklin jabbed at the page in front of them. "It says here we've got to show cons—consy—"

"Consideration," murmured Grimma.

"—consideration for other road users," he said. A jolt threw him forward. "What was that?" he said.

"Us going onto the sidewalk! Right! *Right!*"

Masklin caught a brief glimpse of a brightly lit

store window before the truck hit it sideways and bounced back onto the street in a shower of glass.

"Now left, now left, now right, right! Straight! Left, I said *left!*" Angalo peered at the bewildering pattern of lights and shapes in front of them.

"There's another street here," he said. "Left! Give me left! Lots and lots of left! More left than that!"

"There's a sign," said Masklin helpfully.

"Left!" shrieked Angalo. "Now right. Right! Right!"

"You wanted left," said the signaler accusingly.

"And now I want right! Lots of right! Duck!"

"We haven't got a signal for—"

This time *whoomph* wouldn't have done. It was definitely *bang!* The truck hit a wall, ground along it in a spray of sparks, rolled into a pile of garbage cans, and stopped.

There was silence, except for little hissing sounds and *pink, pink* noises from the engine.

Then Dorcas's voice came up from the darkness, slow and full of menace. "Would you mind telling us down here," it said, "what you're doing up there?"

"We'll have to think of a better way of steering," Angalo called down. "And lights. There should be a switch somewhere for lights."

Masklin struggled to his feet. The truck appeared to be stuck in a dark, narrow street. There were no lights anywhere.

He helped Gurder stand up and brushed him down. The Stationeri looked bewildered.

"We're there?" he said.

"Not quite," said Masklin. "We've stopped to, er, work out a few things. While they're doing that I think we'd better go back and check that everyone's all right. They must be getting pretty worried. You come, too, Grimma."

They climbed down and left Angalo and Dorcas deep in argument about steering, lights, clear instructions, and the need for a proper supply of all three.

There was a gabble of voices in the back of the truck, mixed with the crying of babies. Quite a few nomes had been bruised by the throwing about, and Granny Morkie was tying a splint to the broken leg of a nome who had been caught by a falling box when they hit the wall.

"Wee bit rougher than the last time," she commented dryly, tying a knot in the bandage. "Why've we stopped?"

"Just to sort out a few things," said Masklin, trying to sound more cheerful than he felt. "We'll be moving again soon. Now that everyone knows what to expect." He gazed down the dark shadowy length of the truck, and inquisitiveness overcame him.

"While we're waiting, I'm going to take a look outside," he said.

"What on earth for?" said Grimma.

"Just to, you know, look around," said Masklin awkwardly. He nudged Gurder. "Want to come?" he asked.

"What? Outside? Me?" The Stationeri looked terrified.

"You'll have to sooner or later. Why not now?"

The Stationeri hesitated for a moment, and then shrugged.

"Will we be able to see the Store"—he licked his dry lips—"from the *Outside*?" he said.

"Probably. We really haven't gone very far," said Masklin.

"Will there be foxes?"

"I shouldn't think so," said Masklin as diplomatically as he could.

A team of nomes helped them over the back of the truck and they swung down onto what Gurder would almost certainly have called the floor. It was damp, and a fine spray hung in the air. Masklin breathed deeply. This was Outside, all right. Real air, with a slight chill to it. It smelled fresh, not as though it had been breathed by thousands of nomes before him.

"The sprinklers have come on," said Gurder.

"The what?"

"The sprinklers," said Gurder. "They're in the ceiling, you know, in case of f—" He stopped and looked up. "Oh, my," he said.

"I think you mean the rain," said Masklin.

"Oh, my."

"It's just water coming out of the sky," said Masklin. He felt something more was expected of him. "It's wet," he added, "and you can drink it. Rain. You don't have to have pointy heads. It just rolls off anyway."

"Oh, my."

"Are you all right?"

Gurder was trembling. "There's no roof!" He moaned. "And it's so big!"

Masklin patted him on the shoulder.

"Of course all this is new to you," he said. "You mustn't worry if you don't understand everything."

"You're secretly laughing at me, aren't you?" said Gurder.

"Not really. I know what it's like to feel frightened."

Gurder pulled himself together. "Frightened? Me? Don't be foolish. I'm quite all right," he said. "Just a little, er, surprised. I, er, wasn't expecting it to be quite so, quite so, quite so *outside*. Now I've had time to come to terms with it, I feel much better. Well, well. So this is what it's like"—he turned the word around his tongue like a new sour ball—"Outside. So, er, big. Is this all of it or is there any more?"

"Lots," said Masklin. "Where we lived, there was nothing but Outside to start with."

Masklin turned and looked up at the truck. It

was almost wedged in an alley littered with trash. There was a large dent in the end of it.

The opening at the far end of the alley was bright with streetlights in the drizzle. As he watched a vehicle swished by with a blue light flashing. It was singing. He couldn't think of any other word to describe it.

"How odd," said Gurder.

"It used to happen sometimes at home," said Masklin. It was secretly rather pleasing, after all this time, to be the one who knew things. "You'd hear ones go along the highway like that. Woo-woo woo-woo WOO-WOO WOO-WOO woo-wow. I think it's just to make people get out of the way."

They crept along the gutter and craned to look over the sidewalk at the corner just as another bawling car hurtled past.

"Oh, Bargains Galore!" said Gurder, and put his hands over his mouth.

The Store was on fire. Flames fluttered at some of the upper windows like curtains in a breeze. A pall of smoke rose gently from the roof and made a darker column against the rainy sky.

The Store was having its last sale. It was holding a Grand Final Clearance of specially selected sparks and flames to suit every pocket.

Humans bustled around in the street below it. There were a couple of trucks with ladders on them. It looked as though some were spraying water into the building.

Masklin looked sidelong at Gurder, wondering what the nome was going to do. In fact, he took it a lot better than Masklin would have believed, but when he spoke it was in a wound-up way, as if he was trying to keep his voice level.

"It's . . . it's not how I imagined it," he croaked.

"No," said Masklin.

"We . . . we got out just in time."

"Yes."

Gurder coughed. It was as if he'd just had a long debate with himself and had reached a decision. "Thanks to Arnold Bros. (est. 1905)," he said firmly.

"Excuse me?"

Gurder stared at Masklin's face. "If he hadn't called you to the Store, we'd all still be in there," he said, sounding more confident with every word.

"But . . ." Masklin paused. That didn't make any sense. If they hadn't left, there wouldn't have been a fire. Would there? Hard to be sure. Maybe some fire had got out of a fire bucket. Best not to argue. There were some things people weren't happy to argue about, he thought. It was all very puzzling.

"Funny he's letting the Store burn," he said.

"He didn't have to," said Gurder. "There's the sprinklers, and there's these special things to make the fire go out. Fire Exits, they're called. But he let the Store burn because we don't need it anymore."

There was a crash as the entire top floor fell in on itself.

"There goes Consumer Accounts," said Masklin. "I hope all the humans got out."

"Who?"

"You know. We saw their names on the doors. Salaries. Accounts. Personnel. General Manager," said Masklin.

"I'm sure Arnold Bros. (est. 1905) made arrangements," said Gurder.

Masklin shrugged. And then he saw, outlined against the firelight, the figure of Prices Slashed. There was no mistaking that hat. He was even holding his flashlight, and he was deep in conversation with some other humans. When he half turned Masklin saw his face. He looked very angry.

He also looked very human. Without the terrible light, without the shadows of the Store at night, Prices Slashed was just another human.

On the other hand . . .

No, it was too complicated. And there were more important things to do.

"Come on," he said. "Let's get back. I think we should get as far away as possible as quickly as we can."

"I shall ask Arnold Bros. (est. 1905) to guide us and lead us," said Gurder firmly.

"Yes, good," said Masklin, "good idea. And why not? But now we really must—"

"Has his sign not said If You Do Not See What You Require, Please Ask?" said Gurder.

Masklin took him firmly by the arm. Everyone needs something, he thought. And you never know.

"I pull this string," said Angalo, indicating the thread over his shoulder and the way it disappeared down into the depths of the cab, "and the leader of the steering wheel left-pulling team will know I want to turn left. Because it's tied to his arm. And this other one goes to the right-pulling team. So we won't need so many signals and Dorcas can concentrate on the gears and things. And the brakes. After all," he added, "we can't always rely on having a wall to run into when we want to stop."

"What about lights?" said Masklin. Angalo beamed.

"Signal for the lights," he said to the nome with flags. "What we did was, we tied threads to switches—"

There was a click. A big metal arm moved across the windshield, clearing away the raindrops. They watched it for a while.

"Doesn't really *illuminate* much, does it?" said Grimma.

"Wrong switch," muttered Angalo. "Signal to leave the wipers on but put on the *lights.*"

There was some muffled argument below them,

and then another click. Instantly the cab was filled with the dull throbbing sound of a human voice.

"It's all right," said Angalo. "It's only the radio. But it's not the *lights*, tell Dorcas."

"I know what a radio is."

"What is it, then?" said Masklin, who didn't know.

"Twenty-Nine Ninety-Five, Batteries Extra," said Gurder. "With AM, FM, and Auto-Reverse Cassette. Bargain Offer, Not to Be Repeated."

"Am and Fum?" said Masklin.

"Yes."

The radio voice boomed on:

"—ggest fire in the town's history, with firemen coming in from as far afield as Newtown. Meanwhile, police are searching for one of the store's trucks, last seen leaving the building just before—"

"The lights. The *lights*. Third switch along," said Angalo. There was a few seconds pause, and then the alley in front of the truck was bathed in white light.

"There should be two, but one got broken when we left the Store," said Angalo. "Well, then, are we ready?"

". . . Anyone seeing the vehicle should contact Grimethorpe police on—"

"And turn off the radio," said Angalo. "That mooing gets on my nerves."

"I wish we could understand it," said Masklin. "I'm sure they're fairly intelligent, if only we could understand it."

He nodded at Angalo. "Okay," he said. "Let's go."

It seemed much better this time. The truck scraped along the wall for a moment and then came free and moved gently down the narrow alley toward the lights at the far end. As the truck came out from between the dark walls Angalo called for the brakes, and it stopped with only a mild jolt.

"Which way?" he asked. Masklin looked blank.

Gurder fumbled through the pages of the diary. "It depends on which way we're going," he said. "Look for signs saying, er, Africa. Or Canada, perhaps."

"There's a sign," said Angalo, peering through the rain. "It says Town Center. And then there's an arrow and it says"—he squinted—"Onny—"

"One Way Street," murmured Grimma.

"Town Center doesn't sound like a good idea," said Masklin.

"Can't seem to find it on the map, either," said Gurder.

"We'll go the other way, then," said Angalo, hauling on a thread.

"And I'm not sure about One Way Street," said Masklin. "I think you should only go along it one way."

"Well, we are," said Angalo smugly. "We're going *this* way."

The truck rolled out of the side street and bumped neatly onto the sidewalk.

"Let's have a second gear," said Angalo. "And a bit more go-faster pedal." A car swerved slowly out of the truck's way, its horn sounding—to nome ears—like the lost wail of a foghorn.

"Shouldn't be allowed on the road, drivers like that," said Angalo. There was a thump, and the remains of a streetlight bounced away. "And they put all this stupid stuff in the street too," he added.

"Remember to show consideration for other road users," said Masklin severely.

"Well, I am, aren't I? I'm not running into them, am I?" said Angalo. "What was that thump?"

"Some bushes, I think," said Masklin.

"See what I mean? Why do they put things like that in the street?"

"I think the street is more sort of over to your right," said Gurder.

"And it moves around as well," said Angalo sullenly, pulling the right-hand string slightly.

It was nearly midnight, and Grimethorpe was not a busy town after dark. Therefore there was no one rushing to run into the truck as it slid out of Alderman Surley Way and roared up John Lennon Avenue, a huge and rather battered shape under the yellow sodium glare. The rain had stopped, but there were wisps of mist coiling across the street.

It was almost peaceful.

"Right, third gear," said Angalo, "and a bit faster. Now, what's that sign coming up?"

Grimma and Masklin craned to see.

"Looks like Road Works Ahead," said Grimma in a puzzled voice.

"Sounds good. Let's have some more fast, down there."

"Yes, but," said Masklin, "why say it? I mean, you could understand Road *Doesn't* Work Ahead. Why tell us it works?"

"Maybe it means they've stopped putting curbs and lights and bushes in it," said Angalo, "Maybe—"

Masklin leaned over the edge of the platform.

"Stop!" he shouted. "Lots and lots of stop!"

The Brake Pedal team looked up in astonishment, but obeyed. There was a scream from the tires, yells from the nomes who were thrown forward, and then a lot of crunching and clanging from the front of the truck as it skidded through an assortment of barriers and cones.

"There had better," said Angalo, when it had finally stopped, "be a very good reason for that."

"I've hurt my *knee*," said Gurder.

"There isn't any more street," said Masklin simply.

"Of course there's street," snapped Angalo. "We're on it, aren't we?"

"Look down. That's all. Just look down," said Masklin.

Angalo peered down at the street ahead. The most interesting thing about it was that it wasn't there. Then he turned to the signaler.

"Can we please have just a wee bit of backward," he said quietly.

"A smidgen?" said the signaler.

"And none of your backtalk," said Angalo.

Grimma was also staring at the hole in the street. It was big. It was deep. A few pipes lurked in the depths.

"Sometimes," she said, "I think humans really don't understand anything about the proper use of language."

She leafed through the Code as the truck was reversed carefully away from the pit and, after crushing various things, driven onto the grass until the street was clear.

"It's time we were sensible about this," she said. "We can't assume anything means what it says. So go slow."

"I was driving perfectly safely," said Angalo sulkily. "It's not my fault if things are all wrong."

"So go slow, then."

They stared in silence at the rolling road.

Another sign loomed up.

Masklin peered through the damp air.

"It says," he said, "that it's Slippery When Wet."

"Hooray," said Angalo sarcastically.

There was silence. Then Masklin said, "Shouldn't we do something about that?"

"Why?" said Angalo. "What's it to us? So the sign is slippery when it's wet, it's a slippery sign. What do you want to do, go back and give it a wash?"

"I think perhaps you should be careful," said Masklin.

"And look at the road more," said Grimma.

"I *am* looking," snapped Angalo. "And I'm being careful. Let's have a bit more speed down there! Lots more fast!"

"I think the sign was trying to tell us the *road* is slippery when wet," said Masklin as the truck surged forward.

Angalo looked sideways at him "Oh?" he snarled. "So you tell me: *how does it know?*"

"Angalo—" said Grimma urgently.

"What now?" he growled.

"There isn't any road!"

In fact, there was plenty of road. But most of it was curving around to the right. The truck, on the other hand, was not curving around to the right. It was still going straight ahead.

"Stop!" Angalo shouted.

There was a shudder, and a screeching noise.

"I said stop!"

"We've giving all the brakes we've got!" Dorcas shouted up. "There aren't any more!"

There was a brief *whee-OWWww* as a car flashed past them. Then the truck hit the bank, bounced up it, uprooted a lot of fencing, thumped across a piece of plowed field, and then teetered down another bank and onto the road again. It rolled to a halt.

There was silence in the cab again. Then someone groaned.

Masklin crawled to the edge of the platform and looked down into the frightened face of Gurder, who was hanging on to the edge.

"What happened?" He groaned.

Masklin hauled him back up to safety and dusted him off.

"I think," he said, "that sometimes the signs mean what they say."

Grimma pulled herself out from underneath the Code. Angalo untangled himself from lengths of string and found himself looking into her furious scowl.

"You," she said, "are a total idiot. And speed mad! Why don't you *listen*?"

"You can't speak to me like that!" said Angalo, cowering back. "Gurder, tell her she can't call me names like that!"

Gurder sat trembling on the edge of the platform.

"As far as I am concerned right now," he said, "she can call you what she likes. Go to it, young woman."

Angalo glowered. "Hold on," he said. "I was doing fine until you all started shouting at me! You got me all confused!"

Gurder waved a finger at him. "Don't you shout at me—" he began.

"And don't you 'young woman' me in that tone of voice!" screamed Grimma.

Dorcas's voice came up from the depths.

"I don't want to interrupt anything," it said, "but if this happens one more time, there are people down here who will be getting very angry. Is that understood?"

"Just a minor steering problem," Masklin called down cheerfully. He turned back to the others.

"Now you all look here," he said quietly. "This arguing has got to stop. Every time we hit a problem we start bickering. It's not sensible."

Angalo sniffed. "We were doing perfectly all right until he—"

"*Shut up!*"

They stared at him. He was shaking with anger.

"I've had just about enough of all of you!" he shouted. "You make me ashamed! We were doing so well! I haven't spent ages trying to make all this happen just for a, a, a *steering committee* to ruin it all! Now you can all get up and get this thing moving again! There's a whole truckload of nomes

back there! They're depending on you! Understand?"

They looked at one another. They stood up
sheepishly. Angalo pulled up the steering strings.
The signaler untangled his flags.

"Ahem," said Angalo quietly. "I think . . .
yes, I think a little bit of first gear might be in
order here if it's all the same to everybody?"

"Good idea. Go ahead," said Gurder.

"But carefully," said Grimma.

"Thank you," said Angalo politely. "Is that all
right by you, Masklin?" he added.

"Hmm? Yes. Yes. Fine. Go."

At least there were no more buildings. The
truck purred along the lonely road, its one remaining headlight making a white glow in the mist.
One or two vehicles passed them on the other side
of the highway.

Masklin knew that soon they should be looking
for somewhere to stop. It would have to be somewhere sheltered, away from humans—but not too
far away because he was pretty certain there were
still plenty of things the nomes were going to need.
Perhaps they were going north, but if they were it
would be sheer luck.

It was at that moment—tired, angry, and with
his mind not entirely on what was in front of him
—that he saw Prices Slashed.

There was no doubt about it. The human was
standing in the road waving his flashlight. There

was a car beside him, with a blue flashing light on top.

The others had seen it too.

"Prices Slashed!" Gurder moaned. "He's got here ahead of us!"

"More speed," said Angalo grimly.

"What are you going to do?" said Masklin.

"We'll see how his light can stand up to a truck!" muttered Angalo.

"You can't do that! You can't drive trucks into people!"

"It's Prices Slashed!" said Angalo. "It's not people!"

"He's right," said Grimma. "*You* said we mustn't stop now!"

Masklin grabbed the steering strings and gave one a yank. The truck skewed around just as Prices Slashed dropped his flashlight and, with respectable speed, jumped into the hedge. There was a bang as the rear of the truck hit the car, and then Angalo had the threads again and was guiding them back into something like a straight line.

"You didn't have to do that," he said sullenly. "It's all right to run into Prices Slashed, isn't it, Gurder?"

"Well. Er," said Gurder. He gave Masklin an embarrassed look. "I'm not sure it *was* Prices Slashed, in fact. He had darker clothes, for one thing. And the car with the blue light on it."

"Yes, but he had the peaked hat and the terrible light!"

The truck bumped off a bank, taking away a large chunk of soil, and lurched back into the road.

"Anyway," said Angalo in a satisfied voice, "that's all behind now. We left Arnold Bros. (est. 1905) behind in the Store. We don't need that stuff. Not Outside."

Noisy though it was in the cab, the words created their own kind of silence.

"Well, it's true," said Angalo defensively. "And Dorcas thinks the same thing. And a lot of the younger nomes."

"We shall see," said Gurder. "However, I suspect that if Arnold Bros. (est. 1905) was ever anywhere, then he's everywhere."

"What do you mean by that?"

"I'm not sure myself. I need to think about it."

Angalo sniffed. "Well, think about it, then. But I don't believe it. It doesn't matter anymore. May Bargains Galore turn against me if I'm wrong," he added.

Masklin saw a blue light out of the corner of his eye. There were mirrors over the wheels of the truck, and although one of them was smashed and the other one was bent, they still worked after a fashion. The light was behind the truck.

"He's coming after us, whoever it is," he said mildly.

"And there's that woo-woo, woo-woo noise,"
said Gurder.

"I think," Masklin went on, "that it might be a
good idea to get off this road."

Angalo glanced from side to side.

"Too many hedges," he said.

"No, I meant onto another road. Can you do
that?"

"Ten-four. No problem. Hey, he's trying to
overtake! What a nerve! Ha!" The truck swerved
violently.

"I wish we could open the windows," he
added. "One of the drivers I watched, if anyone
behind him honked, he'd wave his hand out of the
window and shout things. I think that's what
you're supposed to do. He waved his arm up and
shouted, '*Yahgerronyerr.*'"

"Don't worry about that. Just find another
road, a small road," said Masklin soothingly. "I'll
be back in a minute."

He lowered himself down the swaying ladder
to Dorcas and his people. There wasn't too much
going on at the moment, just little tugs on the big
wheel from the steering groups and a steady pressure on the go-faster pedal. Many of the nomes
were sitting down and trying to relax. There was a
ragged cheer when Masklin joined them.

Dorcas was sitting by himself, scribbling
things on a piece of paper.

"Oh, it's you," he said. "Everything working now? Have we run out of things to bump into?"

"We're being followed by someone who wants to make us stop," said Masklin.

"Another truck?"

"A car, I think. With humans in it."

Dorcas scratched his chin.

"What do you want me to do about it?"

"You used things to cut the truck wires when you didn't want it to go," said Masklin.

"Pliers. What about them?"

"Have you still got them?"

"Oh, yes. But you need two nomes to use them."

"Then I shall need another nome." Masklin told Dorcas what he had in mind.

The old nome looked at him with something like admiration, and then shook his head.

"It'll never work," he said. "We won't have the time. Nice idea, though."

"But we're so much faster than humans! We *could* do it and be back at the truck before they know!"

"Hmm." Dorcas grinned nastily. "You going to come?"

"Yes. I, er, I'm not sure nomes who've never been outside the Store will be able to cope."

Dorcas stood up and yawned. "Well, I'd like to try some of this 'fresh air' stuff," he said. "I'm told it's very good for you."

•

If there had been watchers peering over the hedge into that mist-wreathed country road, they would have seen a truck come thundering along at quite an unsafe speed.

They might have thought, That's an unusual vehicle, it seems to have lost quite a few things it should have, like one headlight, a bumper, and most of the paint down one side, and picked up a number of things it shouldn't have, like some pieces of bush and more dents than a sheet of corrugated metal.

They might have wondered why it had a Road Works Ahead sign hanging from one door handle.

And they would certainly have wondered why it rolled to a stop.

The police car behind it stopped rather more impressively, in a shower of gravel. Two men almost fell out of it and ran to the truck, wrenching open the doors.

If the watchers had been able to understand Human, they'd have heard someone say "All right, buddy, that's it for tonight" and then say "Where's he gone? There's just a load of string in here!" And then someone else would say "I bet he's jumped out and hotfooted it over the fields."

And while this was going on, and while the policemen poked vaguely in the hedge and shone their flashlights into the mist, the watchers might have noticed a couple of very small shadows run out from under the rear of the truck and disappear under the car. They moved very fast, like mice. Like mice, their voices were high-pitched, fast, and squeaky.

They were carrying a pair of pliers.

A few seconds later they scurried back again. And, almost as soon as they'd disappeared under the truck, it started up.

The men shouted and ran back to their car.

But instead of roaring into life, it went *whir, whir, whir* in the misty night.

After a while one of them got out and lifted the hood.

As the truck vanished into the mist, its single rear light a fading glow, he knelt down, reached under the car, and held up a handful of neatly cut wires. . . .

This is what the watchers would have seen. In fact, the only watchers were a couple of cows, and they didn't understand any of it.

Perhaps it nearly ends there.

A couple of days later the truck was found in a ditch some way outside the town. What was stranger was this: The battery, and every wire, light bulb, and switch, had been taken out of it. So had the radio.

The cab was full of bits of string.

Fourteen

XV. And the nomes said, Here is a new Place, to be ours for Ever and Ever.

XVI. And the Outsider said nothing.

—From The Book of Nome, Exits Chap. 4, v. XV–XVI

It had been a quarry. The nomes knew this because the gate had a rusty sign on it: Quarry. Dangerous. Do Not Enter.

They found it after a mad, panicked run across the fields. By luck, if you listened to Angalo. Because of Arnold Bros. (est. 1905), if you believed Gurder.

It doesn't matter how they settled in, found the few old tumbledown buildings, explored the caves and rock heaps, cleared out the rats. That wasn't too difficult. The harder part was persuading most of the older nomes to go Outside; they felt happier with a floor over their heads. Granny Morkie came in useful there. She made them watch her walk up and down Outside, braving the terrible Fresh Air.

Besides, the food taken from the Store didn't last forever. There was hunger, and there were rabbits in the fields above. Vegetables, too. Not nice and clean, of course, as Arnold Bros. (est. 1905) had intended they should be, but just sticking in the ground and covered with dirt. There were complaints about this. The molehills that appeared in a nearby field were simply the result of the first experimental potato mine. . . .

After a couple of nasty experiences, foxes learned to keep away.

And then there was Dorcas's discovery of electricity, still in wires leading to a box in one of the deserted sheds. Getting at it while staying alive seemed to need nearly as much planning as the Great Drive, with a lot of broom handles and rubber gloves involved.

After a lot of thought Masklin had pushed the Thing near one of the electric wires. It had flashed a few lights but had kept silent. He felt it was listening. He could *hear* it listening.

He'd taken it away again and tucked it into a gap in one of the walls. He had an obscure feeling that it wasn't time to use the Thing yet. The longer they left it, he thought, the longer they'd have to work out for themselves what it was they were doing. He'd like to wake it up later and say, Look, this is what we've done, all by ourselves.

Gurder had already worked out that they were probably somewhere in China.

And so the year turned, and spring became summer. . . .

But it wasn't finished, Masklin felt.

He sat on the rocks above the quarry, on guard. They always kept a guard on duty, just in case. One of Dorcas's inventions, a switch that was connected to a wire that would light a bulb down under one of the sheds, was hidden under a stone by his side. He'd been promised radio, one of these days. One of these days might be quite soon because Dorcas had pupils now. They seemed to spend a lot of time in one of the tumbledown sheds, surrounded by bits of wire and looking very serious.

Guard duty was quite popular, at least on sunny days.

This was home now. The nomes were settling in, filling in the corners, planning, spreading out, starting to *belong*.

Especially Bobo. He'd disappeared on the first day and turned up again much later, scruffy and proud, as the leader of the quarry rats and father of a lot of little ratlings. Perhaps it was because of this that the rats and the nomes seemed to be getting along okay, politely avoiding each other whenever possible and not eating one another.

They belong here more than we do, thought

Masklin. This isn't really our place. This place be-
longs to humans. They've just forgotten about it
for a while, but one day they'll remember it.
They'll come back here and we'll have to move on.
We'll always have to move on. We'll always try to
create our own little worlds inside the big world.
We used to have it all, and now we think we're
lucky to have a little part.

He looked down at the quarry below him. He
could just make out Grimma sitting in the sun
with some of the young nomes, teaching them to
read.

That was a good thing, anyway. He'd never be
that good at reading, but the kids seemed to pick it
up easily enough.

But there were still problems. The departmental families, for example. They had no departments
to rule and spent a lot of time squabbling. There
seemed to be arguments going on the whole time,
and everyone expected *him* to sort them out. It
seemed the only time nomes acted together was
when they had something to occupy their
minds. . . .

Beyond the moon, the Thing had said. You
used to live in the stars.

Masklin lay back and listened to the bees.

One day we'll go back. We'll find a way to get
to the big ship in the sky, and we'll go back. But
not yet. It'll take some doing, and the hard part
again will be getting people to understand. Every

time we climb up a step we settle down and think we've got to the top of the stairs and start bickering about things.

Still, even *knowing* that the stairs are there is a pretty good start.

From here he could see for miles across the countryside. For instance, he could see the airport.

It had been quite frightening, the day they'd seen the first jet go over, but a few of the nomes recalled pictures from books they'd read and it turned out to be nothing more than a sort of truck built to drive in the sky.

Masklin hadn't told anyone why he thought that knowing more about the airport would be a good idea. Some of the others suspected, he knew, but there was so much to do that they weren't thinking about it now.

He'd led up to it carefully. He'd just said that it was important to find out as much about this new world as possible, just in case. He'd put it in such a way that no one had said "In case of what?" and, anyway, there were people to spare and the weather was good.

He'd led a team of nomes across the fields to it; it had been a week's journey, but there were thirty of them and there had been no problems. They'd even had to cross a highway, but they'd found a tunnel built for badgers and a badger coming along it the other way turned around and hurried off when they approached. Bad news like armed nomes spreads quickly.

And then they'd found the wire fence and climbed up it a little way, and spent hours watching the planes landing and taking off.

Masklin had felt, just as he had once or twice before, that here was something very important. The jets looked big and terrible, but once he'd thought that about trucks. You just had to know about them. Once you had the name, you had something you could handle, like a sort of lever. One day, they could be useful. One day, the nomes might need them.

To take another step.

Funnily enough, he felt quite optimistic about it. He'd had one glorious moment of feeling that, although they argued and bickered and got things wrong and tripped over themselves, nomes would come through in the end. Because Dorcas had been watching them, too, clinging to the wire with a calculating look in his eyes. And Masklin had said:

"Just supposing—for the sake of argument, you understand—we need to steal one of *those*, do you think it could be done?"

And Dorcas had rubbed his chin thoughtfully.

"Shouldn't be too hard to drive," he said, and grinned. "They've got only three wheels."

ABOUT THE AUTHOR

Terry Pratchett is the author of the highly acclaimed group of Discworld novels, which includes *The Color of Magic, The Light Fantastic,* and *Equal Rites.* Although these books were intended for adults, they have a devoted following among younger readers.

Truckers is Terry Pratchett's first novel for Delacorte Press and will shortly be followed by another adventure among the nomes.

Terry Pratchett lives with his family in England, where, he says, he grows carnivorous plants and tries to make computers do things they were never intended to do.